PENGUIN BOOKS

THE HUNTER

Julia Leigh is the author of two internationally acclaimed novels, *The Hunter* (1999) and *Disquiet* (2008). Her film *Sleeping Beauty* was selected for Competition at the Festival de Cannes 2011. She lives in Sydney, Australia.

D1043019

Julia Leigh

the HUNTER

PENGUIN BOOKS

PENGUIN BOOKS

Published by the Penguin Group

Penguin Group (USA) Inc., 375 Hudson Street, New York, New York 10014, U.S.A.
Penguin Group (Canada), 90 Eglinton Avenue East, Suite 700, Toronto,
Ontario, Canada M4P 2Y3 (a division of Pearson Penguin Canada Inc.)
Penguin Books Ltd, 80 Strand, London WC2R 0RL, England
Penguin Ireland, 25 St Stephen's Green, Dublin 2, Ireland (a division of Penguin Books Ltd)
Penguin Group (Australia), 250 Camberwell Road, Camberwell,
Victoria 3124, Australia (a division of Pearson Australia Group Pty Ltd)
Penguin Books India Pvt Ltd, 11 Community Centre,
Panchsheel Park, New Delhi – 110 017, India
Penguin Group (NZ), 67 Apollo Drive, Rosedale, Auckland 0632,
New Zealand (a division of Pearson New Zealand Ltd)
Penguin Books (South Africa) (Pty) Ltd, 24 Sturdee Avenue,
Rosebank, Johannesburg 2196, South Africa

Penguin Books Ltd, Registered Offices:
80 Strand, London WC2R 0RL, England

First published by Penguin Books Australia, Ltd, 1999
First published in the United States of America by Four Walls Eight Windows 2000
Published in Penguin Books 2001

5 7 9 10 8 6 4

PUBLISHER'S NOTE

This is a work of fiction. Names, characters, places, and incidents either are the product
of the author's imagination or are used fictitiously, and any resemblance to actual persons,
living or dead, business establishments, events, or locales is entirely coincidental.

THE LIBRARY OF CONGRESS HAS CATALOGED THE HARDCOVER EDITION AS FOLLOWS:
Leigh, Julia, 1970–
The hunter / by Julia Leigh.
p.   cm.
ISBN 1-56858-169-6 (hc.)
ISBN 978-0-14-200002-1 (pbk.)
1. Wilderness areas—Fiction.   2. Extinct animals—Fiction.   3. Thylacine—Fiction.
4. Tasmania—Fiction.   5. Hunters—Fiction.   I. Title.
PR9619.3.I.4417   H86 2000
823'.92—dc21   00-057667

Printed in the United States of America
Set in Joanna

In memory of Jen Smith

The Eskimo have a word for this kind of long waiting, prepared for a sudden event: quinuituq. Deep patience.

Barry Lopez, ARCTIC DREAMS

I

Now the little plane drops and the fat woman sitting next to him yelps and spills her coffee; his tray of food goes flying. With eyes closed he begins to count, one ... and two ... and three: a religious man, he thinks, might now decide to pray. Then it is over, they survive, and as the eighteen-seater settles high above the rift of blue which separates the island from the mainland, the pilot quickly and calmly sends his apologies.

There is nobody to greet him at the airport, no rent-a-car desk, and so no smiling rent-a-car girl. The fat woman, he sees, is being comforted by a fat man with a crew cut wearing a White Power T-shirt. From the small crowd gathered in the lounge he guesses the plane out will be full. He waits outside for a truck to pull his luggage across the airstrip and when it arrives he gathers his pack and bag without delay. The mini-bus takes fifteen minutes to arrive in town: 'Welcome to Tiger Town' reads a sign by the highway, 'Population: 20 000'. As pre-arranged he hires a new 4WD utility, the latest model, a silver Monastery. 'Picked a good day for it,' says a smiling

3

girl and so he too smiles, nods, and then turns to leave before she can start to ask questions.

Soon he is out of town, heading south-west. The last Kentucky Fried advertises a '$4.95 Two Piece Feed'. Smaller towns crop up along the highway, tiny collections of corner stores, antique shops and hairdressers. Paddocks flatten out by the roadside, run into foothills. Where there are sheep, there are mud-brown sheep, and where there are trees the farmers have wrapped them in tin bandages at cow-muzzle height. By one stretch of road he passes a haphazard arrangement of topiaries in odd geometric shapes, no swans or giraffes or poodles, and later he sees a stone cottage full of grinning toy cats. He crosses Tiger Creek, Break O' Day Creek, this creek, that creek. At the next corner store he stops for a coffee: sweet and chemical.

The distances between stores draw out and the road turns to dirt. He checks his map. Eventually he turns off at an unmarked T-junction and when he passes the first hillside pricked with uniform rows of tiny plantation saplings he knows he is on his way. Then come the vacant concrete plots: Welcome to the dead town, once a logging town. Here, people have picked up their houses and moved on. A whole row of demountables has been abandoned, the windows bagged with bright orange plastic. But there is a petrol station, and a cardboard sign propped up in the window says 'Open'. At the sound of his car pulling in, a clutch of scraggly children materialises, with two of the bigger ones on bikes. He serves himself and goes in to pay. The woman behind the counter waits a second before pulling herself away from the miniature TV, then sticks out her hand and refuses to speak. He pays in cash, buying a bar of chocolate at the last minute as a civil gesture.

He drives, turns smooth corners. He practises his story. And who – today – is he? From now on he is Martin David, Naturalist, down from the university and fighting fit. 'Hello, I'm Martin David', 'A little turbulence but otherwise not too bad', and 'Yes, thank you, a cup of tea would be lovely'.

He will drink the tea and assess his situation.

It is almost dark by the time Martin David, Naturalist, turns into the long driveway and parks his Monastery in a raggedy front yard. Although it is summer there is a chill in the air and he needs his Polartech top. Here, a little bluestone house sits quietly on the edge of the rippling flats, and rising beyond the house is the steep dark escarpment which climbs to the Central Plateau itself: the last house at the end of the last road. Once it had been a small working farm, but now the wood-and-iron feed shed and stables have all but collapsed, and the weeds, mainly a sunny yellow ragwort, have stolen the paddocks. Three car wrecks, all missing panels, sit out rusting and all about lie discarded tin drums. To the right of the house a corrugated-iron water tank has been cut in two to serve as shelter for firewood. There is an upright water tank, and next to that a vegetable patch, sprouting purple stalks which might be beetroot. The front windows are shut, draped with rainbow-coloured cotton curtains.

To reach the house a visitor must first pass under a bare

wire archway. In better days, thinks M, it would have been covered with a sweet-smelling vine.

—•—

The door swings open of its own accord. Nobody greets him, and he hesitates, baffled: a supernatural door? Before he can call out a greeting a shiny purple jumble of arms and legs cartwheels down the hallway, ending up on the floor before him in a remarkable display of the splits.

'Welcome!' says the girl, catching her breath. She might be twelve years old, maybe eleven or ten – he can never tell these things. She is wearing a purple lycra catsuit studded with a galaxy of silver stars and her dark hair is chopped very short, just above the ears.

'Hello,' he replies, enunciating clearly. 'I'm Martin David. Your mother is expecting me.'

Another, smaller, child slips out from behind the door. This one, a blond, wears a silver cape over a red tracksuit and has glittery swirls of red paint on his cheeks. He doesn't speak, just stares; he might even be mute. The taller child rolls over and, in one swift move, is up on her feet.

'Hello, Martin David,' she says, also speaking with great care. 'My name is Katherine Sassafras Milky-Way India Banana Armstrong. You can call me Sass. This is my brother, James Wind Bike Leatherwood Catseye Armstrong. Call him Cat, or Bike.'

Quickly, she looks across to the younger brother for confirmation.

'Bike.'

'Hello – Bike.' He is not a children's man.

'Mum's asleep,' continues Sass. 'She said to tell you she'll see you in the morning. But we got your bed ready.'

Bike inspects the stranger.

He collects his bags from the car, the two children keeping a silent escort. The girl tries to lift his pack but is defeated. He knew the woman had two children, was twice lost, but it had not occurred to him that he would have to spend any time with them, actually talk to them. What did he have to say to children? All the best children didn't want to talk, or if they did want to talk, they only did so to gather information. They were spies, children, little murderers. And adults, he remembers, were the enemy.

The portal is so low he has to stoop. Once inside, it's clear there has been a coup. The children have drawn on the walls, as high as they can reach. The furniture has been painted, the carpet too. Colour, bright colours, everywhere. Here a slash of blue, there a circle of red, a curl of yellow. A rainbow house. How could the mother have allowed it? And yes, he sees, they have indeed got his bed ready. The pillow is dotted with pink acrylic stars, and the same paint has been used to run a whirly swirl over his doona. The bottom sheet, he discovers, is a brilliant shade of orange. On the bedside table one of the two has gone to a great deal of trouble to arrange a three-deep perimeter of painted pebbles.

He wonders if there's been a mistake. Perhaps he's in the wrong house. (Could it really be?) He'd been told the woman was reliable, that she could be trusted to manage his base camp, to keep track of his comings and goings, to furnish him with supplies, to – if necessary – raise the alarm. And he knew she was being well rewarded, if his own reward was any indication of the company's generosity. He does not like it, this imprecision, he does not like it at all. But now is no time to make complaints and, unpacking, smoothing his sleeping bag over the orange sheet, he reminds himself that patience – patience is a virtue.

The children are waiting for him in the lounge-cum-dining room: a double room with a fireplace, stone-cold, which serves as a crossroad for all the household traffic. A bowl of steaming rice rests on the table, and a bottle of tamari. The girl looks at him expectantly, excitedly. He takes a seat, mumbles an appreciation about the rice and starts to eat. He has to pick a piece of baked-on grime from his spoon. 'There are fourteen spoons in this house,' says Bike. The giant – for M now sees himself as a giant – the giant doesn't talk while he eats. They watch. After a short while Sass can no longer contain herself:

'Well, so, did you like your room?'

What?

'Oh, yes, yes of course I did, thank you, very beautiful. Mmm.'

Immediately, she knows he is lying. Light falls from her face, she ossifies. Bike readjusts himself in his chair. For the rest of the meal they are silent. When he finishes eating he excuses himself, and asks to see the bathroom. Like the rest of the house, it's a mess. Filthy. A black mould clouds the ceiling and the walls. The inside of the toilet is streaked black-brown. The towels stink. He breathes through his mouth. Without warning he is tired, and wants to sleep.

From the bedroom window he can make out the dark wall of the escarpment, embossed dense and dark against the dark night sky. Soon he'll be there. Now, he tells himself, now he must sleep. When he wakes later, tripped by a forgotten dream, there is still a light on in the house and, somewhere, the quietest sound of children tinkering.

—

Come morning it is raining and the sky is grey and constant, constancy itself, so that he sees it is impossible to gauge when the rain might stop. Today he will climb the escarpment. He dresses quickly, and carefully, planning to keep dry and warm. As the rest of the house is asleep he goes outside to do a quick reconnaissance. He finds a chook pen, another shed, and follows a trail down to a knee-deep creek, startling some quails as he goes. He is about to drink the water when it occurs to him that it might be poisoned by nearby properties; it might even have run through the log dump. Returning to the house he is surprised to find that no-one is up. By his watch it's already eight o'clock. The chooks are well awake, scrabbling around in their sheltered piece of dirt. They seem healthy, and well fed: he spies a little of the remnants of last night's rice. He goes through the back door into the kitchen. This is mess. All the bowls and cups and plates are out of the cupboards, piled up on the long bench, piled on the floor, piled on a small wooden table which sits against one wall. Many of the dishes are encrusted with grey rice and in between the piles are little stupas of decaying vegetable matter. The gas stove is also covered with dishes, as far as he can see the only open space is dedicated to the arc of the microwave door. An upturned milk crate sits on the floor. One corner of a poster reading 'Stop the Road to Nowhere' has peeled loose, and he presses it back against the wall. There is no evident food to speak of; it must be hidden. After a small search he finds half a pumpkin and a few stalks of shrunken silverbeet behind a stack of plates. As he moves he hears the scuttle of invisible roaches. Eggshells crush underfoot. And the smell, the smell almost makes him retch.

The house is quiet; he will have to wake them. He finds the children squeezed into a single bed in a small room off the lounge. Bike is curled around his sister's back, one arm flung over her side. M knocks on the door, then clears his throat – to no avail.

'Good morning,' he says loudly.

Sass wakes. Bike, though still asleep, senses a sea-change and rolls away.

The girl is so tired a thin membrane of sleep covers each eye, lizard-like, and he wonders what time they eventually crawled to bed.

'Martin David,' she mumbles. 'Jack's coming this morning, to show you the way up.'

'When?'

'Said he'd come round some time this morning.'

10

'What time?' he asks.

'Said some time. What time is it?'

'Eight eleven.'

'Yeah, some time soon.' Her eyes close, she rolls around her brother.

'Is your mother home?' he asks, impatiently.

Sass jack-knifes, alarmed.

'Don't wake her! You can't wake her up!'

What is he to think? A sleeping princess for a mother? Time to wake up. He is on his way to finding her when there comes a very faint tap at the front door. As he is the only one out of bed, M takes it upon himself to answer it.

'Jack Mindy.'

'Martin David,' he replies.

Jack Mindy has a reddish doughy face, down-turned blue eyes, and stringy grey hair slicked across his bald patch. He stands just under six foot, with broad shoulders and a barrel chest. If he wanted to, he could have broken the door down. Without asking he enters the house, and heads to what must be the woman's bedroom. There, he lets himself in and closes the door behind him. Inside the room a quiet, gentle, secret conversation takes place.

'Right then,' says Jack as he leaves the room, pulling the door tight. 'We'll be off then. You ready?'

Yes, he's ready.

'Just for the day?' confirms M.

'Yeah, a bo-peep, back by dark. I got food.'

They take Jack Mindy's ute. Jack doesn't talk much as he drives. They are not long gone when he reaches into his pocket and pulls out a couple of boiled eggs: 'Breakfast,' says Jack. M nods a 'thank you' and takes the eggs. After half an hour's silence Jack artfully rolls himself a cigarette and looks to Martin David for a light.

'Been up lately?' asks M, snapping a flame from his lighter and taking advantage of the friendly approach. Jack inhales.

'Last time?' He looks to see if that was what was really asked. 'Last time I went up round this way was to look for Jarrah Armstrong.'

Who? Who was – who is – Jarrah Armstrong? M shakes his head.

'Didn't you hear, then?' asks Jack Mindy. 'Didn't you hear he went missing, end of last summer it was. Was out doing his university work, never came back down. Didn't the university tell you?'

'Different university.'

'Yeah, well, bloody nightmare it was. Search 'n' Rescue went out for two weeks. Not a sign of him. The wife, well, you've seen her, she's been bad ever since. Jarrah was a good man, a real good man he was. My wife, she keeps an eye on things, does what she can . . . but it's not easy. Nasty stuff it was, too, nasty stuff.'

Oh? M waits. But Jack will say no more.

This is unsettling: what else has been left unsaid? And how could they have been so careless as to leave this information out: the sleeping woman's husband is dead, she must be disturbed, and so she cannot be trusted. Should he abort the job? Pull out now while he is warm and dry with a full belly? The company would understand: he could come back later when more thought had been given to the plan. But, no, M understands very well the nature of his assignment, that time is of the essence, that he is not being paid to doubt, that he is not one to give up easily, and that if he were, another man would quite happily step in and take his place. And so he raises his brows, responds with an 'I'm sorry to hear that' twist of the mouth.

Jack turns off the dirt road onto the fire-trail that skirts the bottom of the escarpment. The track is rough and narrow, and more than once Jack has to wrench the steering wheel under control. Branches whip and bend against the windows. They stop by a small stand of blackwood, in what to the unfamiliar eye is the middle of a crowded nowhere. Jack goes around the back and pulls the tarp off the ute, gets out the packs. He tosses M his pack as if it were a bag of apples. A fine rain falls as the two men limber up, M wrapping his hands around his ankles, while Jack keeps his hands on his hips and bends forward from the waist, then tips from side to side and, finally, grimacing, arches back.

'See that yellow gum with the double trunk,' says Jack, pointing, 'remember him.'

And off they go, following a track which meanders to the right of the split eucalypt on an apparent path of least resistance. It's a boot-width wide, and overgrown: growing. This kind of bush takes getting used to, and more than once M's beloved cap is knocked off – beloved because he loves his eyes. In no time the men are well and truly climbing, for now the track cuts straight up, a steep and muddy plumb-line running with water. One hundred and sixty-five million years ago potent forces had exploded, clashed, pushed the plateau hundreds of metres into the sky. Now the two regularly lose their footing, grab hold of ferns to steady themselves. Jack goes first, wielding a machete, placing the sole of his boot flat on the ground with every step. When he has to, he wedges a firm toehold in an exposed tree root, scaly black and wet, before swinging himself up with the aid of a sturdy trunk: moving slowly, surely. M prefers to move more quickly. He lets Jack get a fair way ahead and then catches up, taking the weight of each step on the ball of his foot, his heel never touching the ground. Where it is steepest he scrambles on all fours like a cat, his arms as strong as legs. He and his pack move as one. An hour passes before the first sign of any prior trip appears: a thumb-thick twig broken at ninety degrees. Then, not far on, a black blaze on a cider gum trunk.

'Yeah,' says Jack, 'this is it.'

They cross a thread of creek and stop for water. M gets down on his knees, uses his hands to scoop up the icy water. It is cold and sharp, fresh. He feels his heart thumping. Jack unbuckles his pack and rolls it off his shoulders, letting it fall heavily to the ground. He gets out a plastic food bag and rummages around, pulling out a block of chocolate with gleeful sideshow panache.

What does old Jack think about, as he plods along? wonders M. No doubt the missing man has slunk across his mind. Or is he travelling with his comfy wife still warm in bed? Perhaps it's the bosomy young girl at the corner store, the way she chews her gum and flips through the TV magazines while absently twisting her hair? A hot meal of roast lamb and potatoes, the day's unread newspaper, the gas bill? The glory days, when he took to cutting a track with relish, fearsome and unstoppable? What did they call him then? Cracker Jack, Jack Flash? Or, and this is what M suspects, plodding and savvy old Jack may not be thinking at all.

As for M, he who is anchored by neither wife nor home, nor by a lover nor even a single friend, his mind takes flight, wanders. The track they are on was cut by old trappers. In his study of the area he'd read that a hundred years ago the same ground would have been regularly used by men carrying up to seventy pounds of wallaby and possum pelts across their shoulders. Tiger pelts, too, or carcasses: once upon a time. Up on the plateau more tigers were caught than anywhere else on the island. Those brute men went up in the winter when the animals' fur was at its thickest and there they would camp in scant wooden huts for months – months – at a stretch. Hard days, yes, but days of plenty. Boys would leap at their fathers and beg to join. And he would have done so, he would have begged. He would have lived up in the snow and ice and every morning he would have pulled on his leathers, cleaned his gun, and gone out hunting. Without complaint.

And on the days when he would come face to face with the 'tyger', that monster whose fabulous jaw gaped open at 120 degrees, the carnivorous marsupial which had so confused the early explorers — 'striped wolf', 'marsupial wolf' — then he would, with his father's encouragement, have fearlessly pressed the trigger and exploded the peace. 'My boy,' his father would later say to his fellow hunters hunched around the fire, 'that's my boy.'

But — and here M's thoughts, needing some place to settle, come to rest most comfortably in childhood — what choice did he have as a boy, really? Nothing to beg for. The greatest adventure his father took him on was a trip to the next town's annual rodeo. They left first thing in the morning, and were back the same day by dinner: once a year for three years, and after three years his father, the local doctor, an essentially quiet and steadfast man, decided that they had both seen enough. It's been a long time since he's seen the old man, at least — what? ten years — and it occurs to M that his parents might in fact be dead, done away with. This placebo brings him a sudden and unexpected peace.

He climbs.

The rain has stopped. A toppled snow gum blocks the track and Jack stands aside while M hacks a step into both sides of the giant log. The sound comes rude and loud.

'This is as far as we're gonna get,' says Jack, consulting his watch.

They eat lunch and turn back. By agreement M goes first. This time he does it his way: slipping, sliding, pushing off tree trunks, tearing at ferns, the cool air catching in his lungs, his calves and thighs flexing, eyes alert, feet flying, scuttling wet black rocks, lurching left and right, plummeting down the escarpment, and all the while remaining upright, defiant, as though his upper body were attached to a heavenly invisible string. Now and then he stops to rest. Then off again, leaving Jack behind. When he finally reaches the end of the track he dumps his pack and, after a short walk to cool down, stretches out on the hard ground. On his estimation he can make the descent in three hours. With his head against his pack he lies back and waits for the sun and the old man to slowly, slowly pick their way down.

Jack Mindy drops him back at the house.

'Thanks.'

'No worries,' says Jack, exits.

Never, hopes M, to be seen again.

———

Sass lets him in. Tonight she is in pink: all pink.

'He's here,' she calls back down the hall, without saying hello.

He takes off his muddy boots and leaves them by the door. Still in his rain gear he carries his pack to his room. Thankfully, the bed is just as he left it. He notices a lock on his door and determines to ask for the key later. Only when he has changed into warm dry clothes does he venture into the lounge. A small fire is burning, the room is warm and smells pleasantly of wood-smoke.

And what's this? Sleeping Beauty has risen. He turns to see her sitting at the table, a lieutenant-child on either flank. On the wall behind her is a poster of a unicorn prancing amongst some silver starry clouds, infinite clouds, and from where M stands it looks as if the unicorn is growing out of her head. Below the clouds falls mussed shoulder-length hair, which is the same pale blonde as her son's, and he sees she shares her daughter's sharp cheekbones and pointed chin. Not bad looking. He guesses she must be close to his age, somewhere in her thirties; fuckable, except that through the smoke he can detect the faint sweat-smell of old unwashed sheets. The eyes, too, are there in the faces of her children, at least in shape and colour. Something is different, though, and it takes him a while in the half-light to realise that the woman is doped, that her eyes are red-rimmed and heavy. How she has been occupying herself while waiting, he does not know; there is no book or magazine before her, no television on, no radio playing.

'Mum, this is Martin David,' says Sass.

'Hello,' he says politely, thinking: I am always being introduced.

'Hi,' she replies, mustering strength. 'Hi. Lucy Armstrong.'

'Martin David.'

'Mum's not feeling well,' explains Sass, in an uninterested by-the-by fashion.

'I'm sorry,' says Lucy. 'Terrible headache, sometimes I . . .'

18

Her voice trails off, finds its way. 'Sometimes I get terrible headaches.'

'That's no good,' he says and then adds by way of contribution, 'I had a friend once, had the same thing.'

This remark garners no response. Lucy rubs a long fine hand against one cheek, bunches her skin up under one eye. How long, he wonders, has she been like this? And as he wonders a strange thing happens – there by the fire, from nowhere, it slowly subtly descends upon him: he finds he has cultivated doubt. Has he been sent as some kind of test? Do they want him to succeed, or is this – what? – a fool's mission? Is he expendable? Yes, of course he is: chop one head off the gorgon and another will grow, but – and here is his doubt – has his time come at last? Quickly, before it is too late, he chides himself: Be realistic.

'C'mon Mum,' says Bike, tenderly.

The boy rises to his mother's assistance, gently pulls her up and holds her around the waist as she walks, slides, to her room. A long stocking stuffed with newspaper is pinned to his pants. What is it? A tail?

'Where'd you go?' snaps Sass, leaning forward on her elbows.

Jealous: he is surprised to see the girl is jealous. He forgets his doubt, suffocates it, forgets the mother and focuses on the girl. She is the one, he realises, who he will have to deal with, at least for the next few days. A girl! And a jealous girl, what's worse – but jealous of what? Time spent with Jack? His trip up the escarpment? Surely, surely not.

'Jack and I climbed the escarpment,' he says, shortly. He will not talk about it any more.

But his answer has inflamed the girl.

'Yeah, where exactly – ex-actly?' she demands. 'Did he show you the gum with the two trunks? Round there?'

'You been there?' asks M.

'Yeah, we went there.' Now she is furtive. 'You from the university?' She might be asking him to confess to a crime.

'I am. In Sydney.'

'How old are you? What's your star sign? Do you have a wife?'

What? This, M thinks, is the raw form of prying insistence women later cultivate, but never actually subdue. He wishes the girl would shut up.

Fortunately, when she sees Bike return she is quick to change the topic.

'Want dinner?' she asks.

He is hungry.

'Yes, please.'

'Bike, get the food.'

Without questioning, Bike goes to the kitchen and brings out a big bowl of lukewarm rice topped with boiled eggs and a splash of tamari. Wordlessly, he sets it in front of the grown-up.

'And a fork,' orders Sass.

M appreciates this distinct chain of command, and as he eats he estimates how long the girl can hold the house together. If it were a matter of food and shelter she could go on for months. He read a book once in which three children buried their mother in the back garden and didn't tell anybody for – how long? Eventually they were caught out, yes, but through no shortcomings of their own.

'What animal are you?' He indulges the boy.

'Human,' says Bike sullenly.

Oh.

'Do you like cards?' asks Sass.

The mention of cards cheers Bike up. How easy it is to read the child.

'Cards, well, no, not really.' Now M hurries to finish his meal.

Bike flags.

He has not been long in his room when the door is quietly pushed open. It's the girl, holding something under her pink jumper.

'Mr David?' She is shy now. She passes him a package wrapped in red velvet. 'Take this. When you go up. Take this, you can keep it for a while.'

What can it be? This Trojan gift? Under the velvet is ... a photograph, a colour snapshot. Sass, with longer hair, and Bike, and Lucy – is it Lucy? – yes, looking like another woman, a younger woman bearing a faint resemblance to herself, like a happier younger sister. Standing to her right ... resting his hand on Bike's head ... is – it must be – Jarrah Armstrong. He is smiling into the camera with the assuredness of a Buddha. Ah, it's clear where Sass gets her dark, dark hair. So, this is the smiling man for whom a woman has sacrificed her waking hours; creator of the girl-tyrant and tail-boy. And then he understands: the girl still has hope. Her father is up there on the plateau, lost, yes, but wanting to find his way down. All winter he has been looking for the track, living in caves, lighting fire ... how? ... by rubbing snow-damp sticks together; for food he has had nothing but Bennett's wallaby, the odd pademelon. Oh, he's crafty, her father, a magic man. And – he sees it so clearly now – if only he, the Naturalist, would cross paths with the wanderer and, having recognised him from the photograph, send him on his way, then all will be well again: the spell will be broken, the sleeping princess will awake ... Only a child could nurture such hope, such conviction.

I am a professional, he tells himself. And I need this girl to manage my base camp. She must provide me with food and shelter, and keep a record of my comings and goings. If I am half a day late she must send for help. On no other account should my activities be made known. Anything that will make her more agreeable to my demands is to be encouraged. Her father is dead, there can be little doubt, but she refuses to believe it. If she thinks she needs me, then so be it. She has never needed anybody like she needs me now.

'OK Sass, when I find him, I'll bring him down.'

By mid-morning he is packed and ready to climb. The girl, full of puppy enthusiasm, has served him well: from thin air she has pulled six eggs, some dried fruit and nuts, a block of hard cheese (a miracle), a bag of rice, and an old but edible head of garlic. He'd taken it all, except the garlic. Garlic stinks, an olfactory flare. It is enough food, along with his own supplies, to last this five-day trip. In future he will have to shop in town and fill his own cupboard. But for now it is enough, and enough is plenty.

As a parting gesture, when Bike has been sent to boil the eggs, M takes Sass aside and makes a show of carefully slipping the photograph into a side pocket of his pack. He has even wrapped the red velvet package in plastic to ensure it doesn't get wet.

'There, safe and sound.'

She takes hold of his hand and squeezes it affectionately. Her hand is tiny and warm and burrows easily into his paw. She is no stranger to field-trip preparations, her own father must have gone up hundreds of times, and so she appreciates that pack weight is all-important, that a photograph can be weighed. Yes, the girl is touched: in fact, he has almost surprised himself with the lovely gesture.

Before leaving he ensures there is no misunderstanding. If he is not back by nightfall in five days' time Sass must telephone Search and Rescue. He plans to be gone four and a half days, which gives him a half-day window in case anything goes wrong. On a 1:15 000 physiographic map he has outlined in pencil the area in which he intends to walk. Yes, she can see it, she pockets the map.

'Yeah, yeah,' says Sass. 'Heard you the first time. Five days.'

Bike, who has come out to say goodbye, or – and this is more likely – to make sure everything is OK, stands by and says, matter-of-fact, 'There are seven days in one week.'

At the children's twin idiocy M is half tempted to pull out the photograph, drop it on the ground. But no, patience, patience. Patience is a virtue.

'OK you two, see you in five days.'

'Bye,' says Bike.

'Good luck,' says Sass, grins.

M has no trouble finding the track. His pack weighs 22.6 kilograms and, despite his years of duty, his strength and high spirits, as he climbs he feels every one of them. But everything he is carrying is essential, has a vital purpose. To distract himself he practises a favourite meditation: he runs a mental gear check, starting at the bottom of his pack. When he gets to the fuel stove, nestled between his groundsheet and sleeping bag, he can't help but quicken his pace, lift his knees a little. The fuel stove, the fuel stove, all bright blue with silvery spaceship legs – not to warm his food, no, nothing stupid like that, no giveaway signpost. Instead the fuel stove is his one luxury, for afterwards. After, when it's all done, he'll sit up there and, with all the time in the world, set up his little fuel stove on a flat patch of ground, unearth the one sachet of ground coffee he's carrying, the sugar and the milk sachets, and he will light the gas – come rain or hail – and brew himself one fine cup of coffee. And that coffee, how he knows that coffee, that will be the sweetest finest warmest liquid ever to pass a man's throat. He will sit up there, his stainless-steel water bottle cupped between two cloth-covered hands, as he always does when he finishes a job, and let the sweet liquid slowly ... But, of course, he can do without it. Of course. Not like others he once knew, soldiers who refused to leave for a job because at the last minute they'd misplaced their lucky spoon, or a memento from a past lover or, worse, a dear departed colleague. His coffee manna, he can do without. If asked, yes, definitely, without doubt he would let it go ... Up now, moving through his pack: sleeping bag, paracord, first-aid kit, rifle (disassembled, laid out like jewellery in a titanium box), surgical kit, night-vision, graphite pegs, wire, torch, spare batteries, Goretex ... By the time the mantra is finished he is well ahead and hot enough to remove his Polartech.

He stops to fill his water bottle, to calm his lungs. 'Drink before you're thirsty,' he reminds himself, although the reminder is unnecessary, a codicil to an innate practice, an afterthought. Pressing on, his thoughts turn once more to the missing man, which perhaps is inevitable, now that he carries him on his back. Perhaps not, and he recalls the last time he had cause to carry a man. What was his name? Ollie? A South African, another ex-soldier who had pledged allegiance to the biotech multinational, a member of the New Commonwealth –

Western Transcendentalist and Diamond Dog – just twenty years old and fresh to the game. So fresh that he'd blundered into a trap set by poachers, a primitive steel jaw hidden beneath forest humus and wood debris. Admittedly, it was a well-hidden and neat piece of work, and it might have been a matter of luck as to which of the pair of them had the misfortune to set it off. Crash! Both of them near jumped at the almighty snap of those steel jaws. But Ollie didn't jump, couldn't jump. The steel teeth pierced his boot buttery-soft, embedded themselves into his left ankle. It was hard work, prising them apart. He'd had to use his knife to dismantle the hinge. And Ollie, to his credit, had kept quiet, biting hard into his jacket sleeve. They couldn't stay where they were; a poacher would most likely return to put his catch out of its misery, and if he'd found them there the whole hunt would have been jeopardised. So he'd dragged the boy half a click through the forest, the two of them forming some terrible three-legged, four-armed, bow-backed beast, all the way to a safe resting place. There he laid the boy out against a banyan tree and disinfected the wound – the pain had been so great the boy's eyes had fluttered, fallen – and, when he'd done all that he could, he stuffed half-chewed betel leaf into the boy's open mouth, raised the leg on a pile of leaves so that the blood would not drain into the soil, and set off for help. But he had never thought about the boy when they were doing their awkward beastly dance through the forest. No, he remembers clearly now, he'd been thinking about practical matters: the undeniable trail of blood they were leaving. In the end, he'd left the boy at a local hospital – there wasn't enough time to chopper him out – and later he heard that the leg had been lost, at least, just below the knee.

Ollie, short for Oliver. There was a lesson in that. You could hack your own foot off and survive. A test: my foot is caught in a rock crevice, would I do it myself? Yes, he imagines taking out his knife and stabbing, hacking, at his own ankle. The best way would be to work into the boot, at the point where his tibia ended, to stab through the ligaments and disarticulate the smaller tarsals. He'd have to do it quickly, and use as much force as he could on the first cuts, before he lost strength. The trick, the real trick, would be waiting for rescue.

And now Jarrah Armstrong comes alive: how long did he wait – or did he wait at all? And if he did wait, well then, in what condition? The girl's fantasies were not entirely ludicrous; if the man were only lost, uninjured, there was no reason why he couldn't have survived, even through a blizzard or a winter of blizzards. But winter up on the plateau – all snow and wind and ice – that, he concedes, would be hard, very hard. M countenances another possibility: the missing man did not want to be found. Maybe he'd wandered off to die, like the leopard found at 18 000 feet on Kilimanjaro. Like an old dog. But no, the smiling man in the photograph is not about to die. It's nowhere in his face, not in the way he is fondling the boy.

27

Overhead the clouds hang low and pigeon-grey. It has not yet rained today. By now M has passed the fallen log and soon, very soon, he'll reach the plateau. Up ahead he catches glimpses of sky spattered through the airy treetops, and so he calculates the track there must have flattened out. When he pulls himself up between two stunted snow gums and finds himself on moderately flat ground he is surprised at how suddenly the track comes to an end. Looking around he sees how easy it would be to forget where the track drops off, and so he takes care to tag the area with bright orange strips of plastic. To make doubly sure, he unsheathes his knife and strikes two small blazes into each of the two gums he has just passed between, and a little further on, at regular intervals through the flat scrub, he arranges small cairns and turns down twigs. Beside one cairn he notices a little purple trigger flower, finger-tip big, and delicately, with the end of a fern, he impersonates a bee so that the pollen-laden trigger within the flower is released and swings up to strike the fern. The undergrowth that has run up and over the lip of the escarpment is hard-going. Tea-tree creeps in, with its small rigid prickly leaves, green and shiny, a hardy survivor of the nutrient-starved dolerite plateau. Along the way he keeps his eyes open for any droppings: square wombat chunks, dark wallaby pellets, devil twists full of hair and bone.

He is not far through the eucalypts when he stops to take a bearing, stepping away from the exposed ironstone which he knows can befuddle the most reliable compass. He fixes on a point ahead and a point behind: this is the way he will advance within the field, oscillating short distances between A and B, then B and C, C and D, always remembering what has passed. According to his high-resolution, satellite-generated and computer-enhanced physiographic maps (how beautiful they are), he can expect to break out into sedgeland if he continues at a steady thirty-four degrees north-north-east.

On he goes, and he shakes his head when he remembers his meeting with the middleman, the company representative who oversaw all clandestine operations, the besuited ballast, the family man who ensured things didn't quite fall apart. 'Here,' the middleman had said, jabbing his finger onto a map, carelessly punching a crater into a grassy valley, 'we believe National Parks confirmed the sightings roundabout here. You'd be looking at twenty square kilometres.' *Roundabout*: how that had grated, the imprecision. And when M had protested that twenty square kilometres was unwieldy, the same man had simply frowned at the apparent declension and repeated: 'We have full faith in our source – as I said, the sightings were confirmed.' In all they had talked for no more than fifteen minutes, a thick file was exchanged, and now here he was, pack on his back, headed to the rise on his right one step at a time.

M presses forward, bending from the waist, head down, as if a phantom icy wind had sprung up and reduced him to the stunted, whorled state of the trees around him. He makes his way between boulders, side-stepping the low tea-tree and scoparia, or, where he has to, bending his arms at the elbow to screen his chest and face, then pushing

29

through. On the far side of the rise he gets his first view of the valley floor open and vast before him. It is immense. Beyond the valley is another rocky rise, but also, further down, there is a giant T-junction of sorts, a second green valley running into this one below, so that from his high vantage point what he sees is some sort of – what? Primordial civic planning.

Dumping his pack he feels his rib-cage fly open, spring back on its ivory spine. Inhale, exhale. This is it, thinks M, this is where it begins. First, he buries his fuel stove and coffee stash, marking the position on one of his photographs. He wipes the dirt off his hands and reaches deep into his pack and pulls out his encased rifle. From the lid of his pack he finds some flint and a little swab of cotton wool, then he kneels down to gather a handful of dry twigs. But there are few dry twigs or leaves to be found, and so he gathers a clump of snow grass and with his cigarette lighter he singes this grass, holding it close to him so that he can absorb its scent. From his pocket he retrieves a couple of handfuls of the wombat and wallaby droppings he has collected, squeezes them together with a little water and mixes a stinking paste. He slowly smears the paste all over himself, boots included, until he is not quite human, a strange but not entirely unfamiliar beast.

Now the beast slouches toward the valley, down an easy boulder-studded slope, the smooth legacy of an ice-cap spread over sixty-five square kilometres some 20 000 years ago. What must the plateau have been like before? Ragged and jagged, teeming with animals, giant fauna now extinct.

Only the small and relatively quick had survived: kangaroos, wallabies, thylacines, wombats. But it was not, he knows, the last Ice Age that had killed them, those fantastic giant beasts. Already sixteen, yes, sixteen Ice Ages had passed without dramatic loss of life. What made the last one different was a two-legged fearsome little pygmy, the human hunter: a testimony to cunning, to mind over matter. This thought brings M the kind of comfort and satisfaction another man might derive from leafing through a set of family photo albums. What he is doing is what his ancestors have always done, and done well. Ha! Dear grandpapa, you hairy stinking arm-swinging chest-banging old bastard, you proud and wary wielder of the stone-tipped spear ... But no, M is not quite ready. It will take time to get a fix on his prey, to think like a true and worthy predator. Yet he knows it will come easily, this skill learnt in the schoolyard, rough-hewn at fumbling teenage parties, and finely honed during hand-to-hand dollar transactions ... The girl, that Sass, she was the predator, and the boy, he was the prey. When you look, you can see it everywhere.

As he walks he imagines some kind of monster, a twelve-foot ape-man, crouched behind the next boulder. Other eyes on his back ... and in this fateful reverie he neglects to look where he is stepping, one foot plunging into a pothole. The shock of it causes him to curse out loud: 'Shit!' Thankfully, his ankles are strong and this time, this one time only, he hasn't done any damage. Let this be a lesson, he thinks: the ground up here is waterlogged and riddled with potholes, holes beneath the spongy coral fern,

31

hidden holes throughout the sphagnum. See these tarns around you, these hundreds of watery pockets as far as the eye can see, some no more than a metre in diameter, others drawn thin and long, others again as big as the lakes one finds rimmed with white pickets in square city parks – this ground you tread is only feeble ground and any minute it will be reclaimed. Tread carefully.

He treads carefully.

A coppery flush does not quite break through the clouds. He hears a crashing to his right and quickly turns to spy a wallaby disappearing up into the scrub. It has taken all day to see an animal, although from the recurrent tiny piles of droppings he has known that they were always there; asleep, in most cases, curled up in a favourite lair. Come dusk they will filter down onto the valley floor to search for food. In the future, he will be waiting for them, but now, with the long day behind him, he has no better choice than to stop and find his own sleeping place. First he fills his water bottle at one of the larger, cleaner tarns, and then he turns out of the valley, up the slope, to drier, wind-protected ground. In twenty minutes he has found his spot: flat, dry, sheltered by a large boulder. He sets down his pack and gets out the tent and with the grace of a monk he weeds the patch of stones. In eight minutes his little tent stands strong and high enough for him to crawl into. Kneeling down he opens the fine-mesh fly and rolls out his sleeping bag. He removes his food, water, and torch from the pack and then pushes it to the far end of the tent – no devil is going to rip his pack apart tonight.

Alongside the tent he lays three sticks in the shape of an arrow, pointing in the direction he will travel the next morning. He pulls on his Polartech, his beanie, climbs inside and zips up the fly to keep out the mosquitoes. Three of the eggs have smashed in their plastic wrapping, and so he eats them before they begin to stink, savouring each mouthful, swigging water. Finished eating, he takes off his well-worn boots and inspects his feet. No trouble yet, the plastic superskin on his heels is doing its job.

Dark here comes quickly. He undresses and slips into his silky cold sleeping bag. Up above, the clouds mask the stars and the moon alone glows like a strange and giant pearl. Somewhere, he thinks, cherishing his last thought before sleep, somewhere, out there, the last tiger stands with her back to the rising wind and slowly shakes herself awake.

———

Night has not been kind to him, and he wakes feeling groggy and restless. It is a weakness, he recognises, as he manoeuvres himself out of the bag and into his boots, this inability of mine to sleep soundly out in the field, even after all this time. Why is it that other men can sleep like stones on their first night out while I toss and turn at every sound? It is a weakness: this absurd preference for a springy mattress and soft pillow, for absolute silence. Silence! Tell the wind not to blow across the plains, yes, order the animals to keep still and demand the insects hold their wings ... then you'll have silence. Silence, like dreaming of an angel to come and, with one sweep of a feather-soft wing, turn your tent into a palace. Ridiculous. Foolish. Only time will do the trick – only time will bring better sleep. As has happened before, by the second or third night out he will wake in the mornings with a clear head, but always a little restless. As it is, it will be a good hour or two before he really comes awake. Time heals all wounds, that's what they say. That's what his mother had said when he'd fallen in the playground, when he was tripped in the playground, and had broken his arm and was sure it would never work again and that he'd forever be the class freak, the weird one. She'd knelt over him and stroked his hair and said, very softly, so that he almost couldn't hear her, 'Time heals all wounds'. Only much later did it occur to him that perhaps she hadn't only been talking about his arm, that secretly she'd been nursing her own wound, or had so recently been healed that the memory of the wound, whatever it was, and of time's magic trick, was still fresh in her mind. A broken heart, he'd also heard it said, by those colleagues who wouldn't go on a job without their lucky love-struck spoon, only time could heal a broken heart. Was it true? He doesn't know, but it's something that he'd like to know, in case it ever happened. Not that he plans ever to let it happen – that's where those boys went wrong, they let it happen. And what sort of time were they all talking about anyway? Did sleep count? Or was it only conscious waking hours that possessed the fabulous healing properties ... The woman, Lucy Armstrong, she clearly had her bets on sleep. She would sleep through it – her wound. She would wake up one day and her husband would be gone and her life would have fallen apart all around her and she would take a fresh look at it and see clearly what to do and how to fix it, all without feeling the slightest pain, or perhaps feeling only the faintest trace of pain, only a memory of pain, a mere abstract. It was a brave move, perhaps a reckless move, placing all your money on sleep – she'd want to be lucky.

As he breaks camp and heads back into the valley, to a spot four kilometres as the crow flies, he reminds himself that on this job there is no such thing as luck. Luck is for the unlucky, for those who lack precision. This is not easy walking. There are creeks to be crossed, some knee-deep and icy cold, where boots need to be removed so that the toes can inch along, blindly finding a foothold amongst the slimy creek-bed rocks. There are tarns and bogs and there are boulders to climb. He is not a bird, and so he does as the other animals do – he takes the path of least resistance. When he comes to a talus, which he does, more than once, he doesn't try to assail it, but drops down and walks around the mass of boulders, corrects his bearing and continues. When faced with a myriad of tarns he sticks as long as he can to the edge of the wet flat, and only when he must does he pick his way across. And when he finds a creek running in his direction he walks through it, hops from one rock to the next, always testing his weight first, so that the rock doesn't turn up and tip him in. And it is only when he

35

comes to a deep impassable point in the creek, where sheer rock rises on both sides, that he peels off into the thick riparian scrub and – forgetting time, forgetting destination – slithers his way through in a kind of loop fashion, so that he ends up back in the creek, hopping once more from rock to rock and occasionally getting his feet wet. And when the map shows that the creek will no longer take him where he wants to go, then he looks for an animal pad and follows it, getting down on his belly and wriggling under thorny bush when he has to. The luckless animals are smart and have built a complex lattice of paths between the sheltered rises, the food sources, and the drinking water – all without once, thinks M, feeling the need for 'self-improvement'.

On this tremulous path he keeps his eyes open for snakes, for with the sun now shining he can expect to find one taking advantage of the slim warm open ground of the pad. He looks, too, for any tracks or droppings. He does this not because he thinks he will find much, not today, but because he must start to attune himself. To find a tiger print on the first day – the probability is so low it is not worth contemplating (but possible, yes, and so to be kept at the back of the mind). How long had it taken the National Parks researchers to finally come across the print which had led them to the sighting which, in its own turn, had been passed, or rather leaked, secretly sold to the middleman and thereon to him, M? Despite numerous eyewitness reports over the decades, some credible and some incredible – drunken fantasies and wishful thinking, attention seeking – the tiger had remained invisible. Extensive searches had been carried out, once by the World Wildlife Fund, and other times by private buccaneers and pipe-dreamers. But each time those searching had failed, failed miserably. It was hopeless, said the zoologists, because the animal was extinct: a combination of habitat fragmentation, competition with wild dogs, disease and intensive hunting had forced their demise. But this history does not discourage M: there is always new history to be made. Today he is acting upon new information, so today the hunt begins afresh. What he needs to do now is develop his all-seeing eye, his own godliness.

At muddy bare patches of soil directly en route he pauses to inspect for prints: mostly the deep two-toed wallaby spoor, slammed into the mud, or scurrying devil spoor, or the occasional shuffling wombat. No tiger, nowhere a forefoot separated some prominent distance from its toe-pads; no four toes arranged symmetrically around the irregular, almost heart-shaped footpad with two deep grooves extending forwards from the rear border. The fifth toe, he knows, is raised above the others so that only in the most perfect conditions, on Hollywood Boulevard, would it show. He finds no faint claw marks tipping each toe, no distinctive set of fore and hind prints. Nothing. And the possible lairs, the hollow trees and hollow logs, the caves and rock cavities, they, too, are empty. Does he care? He will keep his eyes open, yes, at all times, but this is only the beginning.

When the thylacine kills, thinks M, she does not expect to run down her prey with a burst of speed. Compared to her namesakes, the 'pouched dog with a wolf's head' is a near cripple, with shortened forelegs and hamstrung hindquarters; more like an overturned kangaroo than a leaping hound. 'A stiff gait' is how trappers once described the running movement; he'd read so in the file the middleman had given him. And now the trappers themselves were near extinct, one or two perhaps whiling away their nursing-home days in a fog of pleasant fantasies, so that – aside from one slim volume, a transcription of trapper tales, both tall and true – with the old brutish men will pass the best first-hand knowledge of their prey: first one, then the other. There is a symmetry to this that pleases M, a peculiar aesthetic, and that he is a part of it, and knows it, only makes the pleasure more exquisite: Ah! his god-eye! . . . No, the tiger does not chase her prey. Instead, she persists. She outlasts. On cold lonely nights she rouses herself from sweet slumber and stands with her back to the rising wind, surveys the valley floor before her. And when a wallaby picks up her scent and flees, running desperately in a wide circle, then the tiger, too, lopes along behind, around and around and around again, until the moment when she cuts the circle, her black-striped honey flanks sucking in and out with the motion of her breathing, and with one snap of her awful gaping jaw she crushes the fleeing creature's neck, crushes all the life out of it before, once more, settling down to feed.

I am patient, thinks M. I, too, can wait. Then it strikes

him that his chances of both success and failure increase the longer he waits – for the longer he is gone, the more likely it is that he will be called away. He quickly logs this in his catalogue devoted to the futility of time, then lets it disappear.

———

On the fifth day he returns, as he said he would. The children do not run out to greet him, as he expects, and he discovers the front door is locked. But the back door is open, and he notices a flat patch of grass where earlier he had seen two bikes. Inside there is no movement, no sound, and he assumes the sleeping woman is still in her bed. The grey screen of the TV, he sees, has – in his absence – fallen prey to the paintbrush and he tries to switch it on, discovering the thing is broken. He changes out of his stinking clothes and rimey boots and takes a hot soothing soapless shower. As it is only eleven a.m., he gets back into his car and heads for the nearest town big enough to support a butcher. He ignores the petrol station, and this time when he reaches the T-junction he turns right, so that now he is headed into foreign, but well-mapped, territory. The next town is marked on his map with a tiny red star. Here a string of shops runs down both sides of the main street. There's Sid's Supermarket, squeezed into two store-fronts, and next to that Flo John's Hairdresser, offering an $8.00 deal on all styles plus video hire and Internet access. Beside Flo's is a chemist, then a takeaway milkbar tattooed with red and white Coke bottles, then the News & Travel & Post Agency. The butcher comes next and is hard to miss. Out on the pavement a smiling pig in the form of a wooden billboard holds a sign saying: 'Now Open – Your Local Butcher'. A green square of chalkboard below the painted greeting is empty – there are no specials on today.

M pushes through a screen of long coloured plastic strips into the store. The smell, all sawdust and blood, immediately fills his nose and lungs. The butcher before him is a young man in black rubber gloves who, like all butchers M has encountered, seems very happy with his job. Behind the counter, up on the wall in a glass box, is a stuffed and glassy-eyed thylacine pup. A piece of rib-eye steak on display is pinned with a white plastic card reading 'Tassie Tiger – $50 000/kilo'. M asks for what he wants, and the young man cheerily obliges, goes out the back to 'see what he can do'.

What does the butcher know? That by studying one hair from a museum's stuffed pup, the developers of biological weapons were able to model a genetic picture of the thylacine, a picture so beautiful, so heavenly, that it was declared capable of winning a thousand wars. Whether it will be a virus or antidote, M does not know, cannot know and does not want to know, but there is no question the race is on to harvest the beast. Hair, blood, ovary, foetus – each one more potent, each one closer to God. And it's the quick or the dead, thinks the stranger in town. His angelic thoughts dissipate and now he's a cowboy – there's a tumbleweed blowing down the main street and if he had a pistol in his hand, he'd twirl it around.

'Here y'are,' says the happy butcher, dragging out a bucket. 'Good riddance. But me dogs'll be cut tonight, I tell ya. That's their grub.'

M loads two heavy plastic sacks slippery with hearts, livers and sheep heads into his car. Then he takes them out, back into the cool clean butchery, and ducks into Sid's Supermarket, where he stocks up on dried fruit, nuts, pasta and cheese. Finished, he cuts across the road to the town's one pub, Ye Old Tudor Hotel, with Bottle Shoppe. Best to have a counter meal, he thinks, considering the prospect of another bowl of rice. The outsider's curse, he decides, is this constant vigilance regarding food.

One Reef 'n' Beef and a beer, thanks mate.

The publican, no stranger to strangers, takes the order with equanimity and delivers it to the kitchen. When he has gone, M spies a cardboard poster stuck in the corner of the long bar mirror: 'To Dave – he had his toes amputated so that he could stand closer to the bar'. He wonders, entertaining himself, if there really was a Dave, and if that Dave had been caught out in the snow, had his toes frozen off while in a drunken stupor, so that there was more to this sign than a comradely joke. Unlikely. He takes a seat with his back to the window and waits for his meal. The steak comes thick and medium-rare, doused in tomato sauce, while the fish, which is unashamedly shark, is crumbed and fried. A sorry sprig of parsley sits between the two. Tastes good, better than other hotel meals he's had. There's a TV on, perched high in one corner, and a handful of old-man drinkers are looking at it, just looking, having long since tired of paying attention.

He has not yet finished eating when the happy butcher, gripping the two plastic sacks, comes into the pub and drops the bloody loot by his feet.

'Closing up shop, mate,' he says, winks and heads out.

'Footy at eight!' calls the publican, affirming, not asking.

'With bells on.'

Back at the house, by now it is well and truly dark, he is surprised to find no sign of the children. Yes, he checks, the bikes are still gone. What can they be doing out there? It's getting cold. He takes the bloody sacks to the kitchen and rests them against a wall. Then he sets about clearing the stove-top, piling all the plates in a corner of the room. The sink, too, he empties, and he disengages a large steel soup pot which he begins to clean. There's no scourer in sight, so he goes outside and collects a handful of gravel. Once the pot is on the stove he heaves up one of the sacks and slides the viscera inside. Bubble, bubble, toil and trouble . . . my treacherous brew . . . He enjoys this bloody preparation: it's childish, he cannot deny it, but there is something tantalising about disgust. He remembers the first time another boy had shown him how to pull the shell off a snail while it was still alive, how he had watched, horrified and fascinated at the same time. Now, as he stirs, he hears the rasp of bikes on the driveway.

Sass strides into the kitchen, stares.

'We're vegetarian,' she says quietly.

He swallows a laugh, stirs. Bike comes in, goes

42

immediately over to the second sack and peeks inside, then jumps back like he's seen a snake.

'It's for my project,' explains M, 'to help me study the devils. When they smell this stuff, they come running.'

'Really?' asks Sass. 'Devils are everywhere, that's what Dad says. You just have to leave a bit of cheese out and they come and tear your tent apart.'

'Our dad got his tent ripped,' says Bike proudly.

'Cheese is better,' says Sass, wrinkling her nose as she leaves the room. 'C'mon Bike.'

She stops in the doorway and spins around.

'Did you –' She freezes, remembering Bike is in earshot.

'Didn't have much luck last trip,' offers M, speaking her secret code.

She thinks about this.

'Maybe next time.'

'Yes, maybe next time.'

Maybe, he thinks, maybe not. When he is done parboiling the purpled hearts and sloppy livers he puts them in the fridge to chill overnight. The second sack he shoves into the freezer compartment, planning to fix it up later. He takes another shower to get the blood-stink off him, enjoys the sharp heat on his back and stands until the water starts to run cold. Tonight he will get a good sleep, and at dawn he will head out again. Wrapped in his towel he knocks on the children's door, opens it and sticks his head in. Bike is standing on the bed with both his arms raised above his head. The girl is crouched on the floor, squatting yoga-style over what appears to be a lady's red winter coat, scissors in hand. When she sees him she instantly stops whatever it was she had been doing.

'Sorry,' says M, 'but I have to tell you I'm going up again tomorrow morning, first thing. If I'm not back in ten days, you know what to do.'

'Yep,' says Sass, 'ten days. So by, what? Saturday?'

'Saturday, good, that's right.'

'OK, Saturday.'

Bike, implacable, still has his arms raised.

'I've written it down, and I'll leave it by the phone. But you have to show your mother, OK?'

'OK.' She coughs, a weak cat-like cough.

'You sure?'

'Yeah-ba-dare.'

'Yabbayup,' says Bike.

'Alright then, well, goodnight.'

'Goodnight,' says Sass, scissors aloft.

'Goodnight,' echoes Bike.

He thinks about moving to the pub, taking a room in – what was it? – Ye Old Tudor Hotel (no 'e' on 'Old'), but the thought of the extra driving immediately displeases him. All those hours starting out, he thinks, wouldn't be worth it. Better to be close so as to slip up and down. Better, too, to keep to myself. At the very worst, I won't be more than a day or two overdue before the girl calls for help. Surely not. She needs me, that girl, no question. And the woman, I'll make sure she gets a copy of my schedule. So, he decides, slipping again into his sleeping bag, savouring the space around him, the soft mattress, I'll stay where I am.

44

Do tigers dream? he wonders. And this tiger, reputedly the last of her kind, what does she dream of? The scent of a mate? Or does she have the same dream he has, the only dream he has or, at least, the only dream that he ever remembers: the running dream, where he is being chased for hours by an unknown foe, where he has to hide in bushes and hold his breath, where the bushes transmogrify and he is forced to run again, where he can't run quickly enough and where, finally, he knows he will be caught and that capture means a blank death, but where – dreams being what they are – the threat of capture dissolves and disappears at the very last moment so that, still sleeping, he knows he has survived and the running dream is over.

———

The hearts, heads and livers weigh heavily on his back. He stops in the creek that heads to his first observation post and drinks copiously. A little further on he stops again, this time to take a piss. And so it goes, stopping and starting, sweating and drinking, even as a light rain falls, until midday, when he reaches the place where the creek is funnelled through a long narrow pass, no more than fifteen metres wide. Here a well-trodden pad runs down one steep slope, across the flat and hugs a short length of the creek before darting across at the exact spot where the water is lowest and two large rocks have collapsed to form a sub-aquatic bridge. On the far side it pops out again, dallies through the flat and, where there is no other choice but to climb again, does so, disappearing up over the ridge.

M turns out of the creek, squeezes through the fringe of riparian scrub onto the springy orange-tinted coral fern, side-stepping potholes and moss pincushions so green they are almost phosphorescent. And where the pad first slinks into the bush he drops his pack, for this is where he will set his snare. He finds his wire, pegs and straight stick as he had left them, thinking: With this patina of rain and dirt they are no longer newcomers and, no longer new, they are not to be feared ... So works the oldest trick in the book ... The thing that will snatch you up into the air has been lying dormant all along. Then he searches around for a sapling, something long and thin and flexible, and in half an hour he has found one. On either side of the pad he hammers in a graphite peg; into each peg a notch has been cut at the height of a tiger's chest. The graphite is smooth and cold and pleasant to touch. He lays his straight stick across the pad, slotting it into the notches so that one end is fixed and the other precariously balanced. Two metres away from the left peg he digs a hole half a metre deep. By the time he has finished he is sweating all over. He buries the sapling, holds it fast, and nimbly fashions a snare loop from the fine wire, which he secures to the free end of the sapling. As well as the loop he ties on a short length of wire with a fifty-millimetre graphite toggle. He bends the sapling down toward the nearer peg and, with surgical finesse, lays the toggle under the trip-stick, across it and the peg. He releases the sapling slowly, slowly, taking care to keep his head out of the way in case the toggle-trigger should slip and the sapling go flying. He does all this quietly, like a tourist in a church, like a tourist who has already seen a hundred churches. That in the end he will probably use his rifle does not deter him; nor is he perturbed that the snares themselves invite trouble, the attention of the park rangers – it is a risk he has to live with. Down on his knees, he lays the snare loop across the pad so that any animal which knocks the trip-stick and releases the toggle-trigger will find its leg ensnared, yanked skyward. He places a loose cover of soil over the snare and wraps some leafy creeper around the trip-stick. Then he cuts a small bough from a nearby young strawberry pine and lays it above the trip-stick, shoves it over the scrub on either side of the pad in the hope that the passing animal will not try to jump the stick but will lower its head to pass beneath the bough. As a final measure he pulls a fistful of hearts and livers from his pack and drops them onto the pad.

There, he thinks, the sweet taste of old. Do you remember, tiger, when you were young and used to follow your mother down the escarpment onto the verdant plains? Do you remember how the sheep would mill around in clusters, doing nothing all day but fattening themselves? And how, when they first smelt you, they would tremble and start, push against one another, bleat? But there was only a wire fence, and by the time they had smelt you it was too late, you had already jumped and made your pick. Do you remember? You were the farmer's scourge, and your reputation went ahead of you: they said you roamed

47

the country in yellow-eyed packs, padded through the night with bristling hair and drooling jaw agape, killing at will. Young women were afraid to go for afternoon strolls in case they crossed your path. You'd drag babies out of their frilly cots and wolf down frilly girls whole ... Really, it's no wonder, is it, that the government of the day offered a one-pound bounty for your hide. Ah, perhaps you were so young then you had not yet been born, had only savoured the sheep (and the girls) through your mother's blood, through her mother's blood. But the taste is there, isn't it, just follow your nose.

He stops himself: this dialogue with the tiger is no good. The animal does not care for talk, or for history or for what passes as history. If the food is there and she is hungry, then she will eat: provenance is of no concern for she does not know concern.

When he has done all he can to remove signs of his incursion, M collects his pack and climbs the steep slope to his observation post. Up in the fork of a peeling gum, where he had stashed it, he retrieves his tent. As the light fades and the first pale stars begin to shine he starts to set up. This does not take long: he has already been here, found and cleared his site. He shoves his sleeping bag inside the tent and pulls on his beanie. From where he sits he has a clear line of vision to the snare and the flat beyond. To relax himself, to give himself a reward, he starts to masturbate, imagining the woman he last slept with, a woman he picked up while on holiday between jobs, who said her name was Jacinta – sexy – but who was slow to

48

respond when her back was turned and he'd proffered a drink, 'Jacinta?' A fake name – it was surprising how many women on holidays gave fake names, away from home and out for a little adventure. Enough – back to her breasts, cut to her wet mouth working its way down his chest. Aim away, until . . . done.

Now, eat. He tests out his latest innovation, the rice belt. All day M has been wearing a light plastic tube around his waist, no thicker than a regular leather belt, filled with rice and a little water. His body heat and the day's agitations should, according to the claims of a colleague who'd spent time in the Arctic, have softened the rice into a sort of porridge. He lifts his Polartech – for the cold has set in – and fiddles around with the opening he had devised earlier, a kind of valve, like on a wine cask. Yes! It works – he sticks his finger into the tube and scrapes the ricey mush off the plastic. But on the first mouthful he realises that the water has only penetrated the outer sheath of the grain, which means he should wait another day, perhaps two, before tucking in. He readjusts the valve and buries the belt back under his warm top. Tonight scroggin, cheese and dried fruit will do.

After his meal he lays his rifle across his lap. If anything crosses the flat, if he's looking, he'll see it. Ah, night-vision – God Bless America. He'll stay sharp, although some time he'll have to sleep. Awake till one a.m., he decides, then sleep. Then sleep.

But the day has taken it out of him and by midnight M

49

is waning; he even finds himself head-down dozing, startled back into consciousness like a schoolboy on a summer afternoon. To keep himself awake he throws off his sleeping-bag cocoon and does ten quick star jumps, gets the blood going. For a moment he wishes he had a companion on the job, someone to talk to in the long hours, and it bothers him that the company had insisted on sending him solo. 'A one-man job,' the middleman had said, in an ingratiating tone that insinuated he, M, was the most capable, and indeed the only man to be entrusted with the mission. Which was bullshit. Two of them would have had a better chance: two pairs of hands to build snares and set traps, two sets of eyes and ears, two rifles poised, or at least, in the long hours, one man awake, one asleep. Yes, it bothers him. That niggling doubt again: Why one, why me? Was it possible the company no longer considered retrieval of genetic material a high priority? Had an office-jockey turned all lily-livered? He couldn't see why – what he had retrieved so far had earnt them, how much? Hundreds of millions, probably billions. The company needed him, in fact, was indebted to him. Who was of more value to a biotech company than a hunter: sampler and ensurer of exclusivity. Inbred thylacine, dodo, moa, mammoth, bunyip, yeti, girls with telekinetic power, boys with an immunity to pain, the goose that laid the golden egg . . . mutations all, this was now the stuff that dreams – and wars – were made of.

These thoughts steer M far from sleep and soon he has turned his attention to the night sky. The unending sky. Infinity – starting right at the top of his head and mediated, perhaps, by a planet. And the stars, look at them, they were not God's little peepholes; no, science had long since squeezed all the gods from the firmament and replaced them with bilious clouds of rock and gas. The woman, Jacinta, she'd been keen to point out the constellations to him – their star signs. He'd said that there were stars behind stars and that a faith built around only visible stars was akin to thinking the earth was the centre of the universe.

The tiger, he wonders, when she sees the stars, does she push them into animal shapes, give them names, and then pull them down from the sky so that she can eat them, make them part of her?

The night-vision headset is heavy, omnipresent, and despite years of experience he still is overawed by the massive change it effects on the world around him, his only world. Everywhere he looks the light of the stars has rinsed the world in a fluorescent yellowy-green, so that he might be suffering from a strange sort of colour blindness, or might even be a star-creature himself, with alien eyes. Down on the flat, two lime wallabies are hovering by the creek, and he guesses they have already drunk their fill.

Sit tight, my plump pretties. Sit tight.

It is possible, thinks M, that the tiger herself is sitting as I am, up on the opposite ridge. She may be eyeing these wallabies, watching to see which of the two displays any weakness. Every three or four days, it is estimated, she will need to kill: so say the scientists who have examined the length of her forebears' alimentary tract. But the farmers – phantom-plagued or otherwise – have different stories to tell, stories of tigers who mauled at leisure, sometimes up to nine sheep in a night. Or, and M thinks this is more probable, she might now be watching as a dog watches a log-fire when resting at her master's feet, with her head on her front paws and belly full. Yes, tonight she may well need to do nothing better than rest.

M methodically scours the opposite ridge for possible resting spots, dark holes beneath overhanging rocks. When he trails his jaundice-eye back to the flat he sees that one of the wallabies is headed for the pad, travelling toward him. Damn! With plenty of bait in his pack he doesn't need a wallaby to spring his snare.

Go! Go! Go!

He jumps up and breaks the night with loud yells, crashes down through the scrub. The startled wallaby turns ninety degrees and bounds away. Its companion also disappears. He has, he knows, scared off everything around him: the drunk at the party who keeps spilling his beer. Perhaps he has scared away the tiger. And this outburst has spread wide its discontent, the sound of his own voice being as alien to him as his vision. If he'd had company, he would have turned and pulled a ghoulish face and joked: 'Sorry mate, don't know what came over me.'

He sits and waits.

Come one a.m. he is back at the tent. His arms and legs, his chest, his whole body right up to his chin is sweet and drowsy with sleep. He is so tired that he is tempted to sleep out, not even bothered to crawl into the tent and remove his boots. But he knows this danger well, the siren call of sleep, and he takes a couple of quick deep breaths to shake it off. The missing man, he thinks, there's a man who would have heard sleep's sweet call. As his body temperature slowly dropped, sleep would have made a little room for herself, gently, gently. He would have resisted, yes, but sleep outweighs even the noblest instincts and in her own persistent way she would have filled him entirely, pushed the life out of him. How soft, so soft, it must have been, that final embrace. The wife, M sees now, is carrying out her own search across the soundless plains of sleep. In her bed she labours and seeks to reclaim what is rightfully hers. She is busy, and should not be disturbed.

Once safely swaddled inside the tent M is quick to relent.

In what seems like no time at all he is woken by a desperate high-pitched keening. The snare!

He clambers out of his sleeping bag, thinking only: Yeah, yeah, I'm on my way. He is not excited, no tiger has ever been known to make such a racket. 'Yip, yip, yip, like a dog, a terrier,' reported one Samuel Riley in 1812, when asked by an English reporter to describe the fabled Tasmanian tiger's roar. Strange, that an animal with such a monstrous gaping jaw should possess so feeble a voice. Exotic! said the newspaper.

He is still half asleep as he makes his way through the limey scrub. On his approach the keening grows louder, more frantic, and soon he has the animal in sight: a native cat, caught by one foot, thrashing around in the dark. He observes for a minute or so, wanting to test the strength of his snare. Yes, it holds fast, and though the cat weighs less than a tiger and is not a real test of the snare, M is satisfied with what he sees. For another few minutes he watches this aerial display, now deaf to the ungodly wails, as if his earlier dreams had turned to wax in his ears. The silvery wire of snare catches the moonlight, flickers; the sapling bends and sways. He lifts his rifle to his eye-piece and takes aim, fires. The bullet strikes the animal in the chest, the explosion echoing like a ring of applause. He walks over to the snare and takes hold of the creature by its bound leg and cuts the wire loose. Hardly looking at the corpse, he swings it into the scrub. Then he sets about rebuilding his snare, with the same deliberation and concentration he had exercised earlier in the day. What good is a poorly set snare, he tells himself: as useful as a hole in the head.

The morning sun has slain the stars and he wakes to find that, for once, the sky is entirely blue. For breakfast he eats some cereal with water and then breaks camp, hiding enough wire for repairs back up in the tree. He takes a shit in the hollow of a rotten log and checks its colour and consistency to gauge the state of his bowels. The morning chores over, he returns to the scene of last night's excursion and finds his latest snare empty and intact. With a little more energy and curiosity engendered after the morning meal he decides to put down his pack and search for the cat. Soon he finds what he's looking for: a sorry carcass, or rather, the scant remains of a sorry mangled carcass. All that is left of the animal is the head, still attached to a dull white spine, and one limp shoulder. The rest has been ripped out, torn off, dragged away. Call in the cleaner. The devils, those shameless scavengers, have wasted no time.

On such a beautiful day, when even the elements have decided to conspire with him, M works at a fast, but painless, pace. By lunchtime he has set and baited a run of four snares. Two of them are on the opposite ridge, by deep dark clefts where earlier he had pictured the tiger at rest. If I have imagined you here, he thinks, nailing a slimy warm sheep's head to an ironbark by way of a lure, then here I should set my snares. My imagination is my companion, my man who does the hard yards and reports back what he has seen. What he dismisses as possible, I, too, shall overlook. And when I catch you, tiger, he will shrug his shoulders and say, as he always does — see, I told you so.

And then M remembers: it is better to hunt by yourself. When his father had taken him out rabbiting on weekends, M had never been the first to call it a day. Wait a little longer, he had pleaded over and over with the good doctor. And not only was his father quick to tire on these trips but he made unnecessary noises, even moved when the furry creatures looked his way. He had no feel for it, his father, no feel for it at all. As soon as he was sixteen and had his mother's blessing, M had preferred to go hunting on his own.

He lunches by a crop of lichen-spotted dolerite boulders on the edge of a tarn big enough to be marked on his map as a lake: one of 'Solomon's Jewels'. A small stand of thousand-year-old pencil pines, of a rich sombre green befitting their age, huddle by the shore, and beyond them a bone-white bare gum has fallen into the water. Another gum, with a trunk swirled like caramel ice-cream, presses between the rocks and serves as his resting post. He takes his time eating, has two eggs and works through a portion of his rice belt. The belt, he decides, is not a great success: the rice is edible, yes, just. Enjoying the sun, he studies the light on the water, how the brown hill across the way has also fallen onto, but not quite into, the shimmering tarn. When he stands he sees that he, too, has been tripped up, reflected, toppled down.

The afternoon he devotes to his beautiful traps. All along they have been sitting two abreast in his pack, and now he pulls one out, gently laying it in the sun. His tiger trap – a variation on other traps he has designed, crafted from a light and unbreakable titanium/aluminium alloy. He digs a shallow depression in the earth, then takes the trap and pushes its spring down with the heel of his boot, so that the catch is clipped to the edge of the plate, taut over the open sharp jaws. He carefully places the trap in the depression, and hammers in the retaining spike. One step on the plate and the catch will be released, the jaws will snap shut, the animal will dance and pull, held tight by the spike and chain. Spikes, chains, crushing jaws: there is something mediaeval about it all, thinks M, as he sets about disguising his handiwork with an overlay of leaves and dirt. At this point he would not be surprised to find himself wrapped in a cow-hide cape.

One day his attention is caught by a ring of blackened stones and he imagines they might have been laid by the local Aboriginal people, in the years before they, the full-bloods, were almost driven to extinction. He remembers reading that the government had once tried to make another island, De Witt, an Aboriginal sanctuary – anything to redress their embarrassing demise. It was a tiny and forbidding rock of a place, shunned by all. And, naturally, the experiment failed. Then in 1936, the year the last thylacine died in captivity at Mrs Mary Roberts's private Beaumaris Zoo, it was again suggested that De Witt Island could be put to use – any tigers to be rounded up and sent away . . . Something tempts M to pick up one of the smooth stones and balance it in his palm, and something again tempts him to put it back.

And so one day passes, and the next. He travels, checks the trembling arrow of his compass. When he comes across a bronze coil of snake asleep on a warm patch of earth he has only to stamp his feet and the snake graciously departs. So fine and unusual is this stretch of weather that the ever-present bush flies and their dull cousins, the fat black march flies, have declared some sort of national holiday and gone to ground. Ah, the sun, the sun . . . By night he sits, keeping watch over a wide stretch of grassy valley floor that forms one long arm of the plateau's four-way 'golden gateway'. And so it goes on, by day setting snares and traps, and sitting at night; each night catching some animal – wallaby, pademelon, native cat – and throwing it back to where it belongs: but nowhere the tiger.

The weather breaks, the clouds regroup with new-found vigour. A heavy and unrelenting rain fills two days with grey darkness and for two nights M doesn't leave his tent. An attendant wind springs up so fierce that the creeks run backwards. But what is rain now? The rain is just rain. Now – now he senses it has happened, the alchemical change which seeps through the bones and leaves a man with faculties so attuned that he is no longer man, is more than man. Now M is the natural man, the man who can see and hear and smell what other men cannot; the man of delicate touch and sinuous movement; the man who can find his way through the bush by day and night, and sit motionless through the long hours with his finger married to the trigger.

━

There is a fresh green salad waiting for him on the table. And a BBQ chicken. Yes, it must be for him: there are four empty plates, four sets of knives and forks, four glasses of water. He pokes the chicken, to find that it is cold.

He takes a long hot shower.

Bike sallies into the bathroom, raps at the glass shower door.

'Mr David, Mr David,' he says, 'dinner's ready.' Then he turns and leaves.

Sass has a smile on her face. Bike, too. The mother is sitting with her elbows on the table and he sees she is wearing a little red lipstick. Whoever has applied the lipstick has done an enthusiastic job: her natural lip-line has been obliterated.

'How are you?' says the woman. 'Welcome home.'

'Thank you.'

They sit a while, looking at the chicken. The woman leans back in her chair, her neck droops.

'Do you want salad?' asks Sass.

'Thanks.' He helps himself. Sass does likewise. The woman rouses herself and serves Bike, then spoons a few leaves onto her own plate. She looks across at M and smiles – how? Lovingly? Could it be lovingly? A mothery smile.

He waits to be offered the chicken. Eventually Sass reaches across the table and tries to rip off a leg.

'Here, let me do that,' says M and using the short blunt knife and fork saws his way through.

'Yum,' says Bike, 'yumba-rhumba.'

'Do you like chicken?' asks Sass. 'Everyone in the whole world likes chicken. Jack brought it round today.'

'Mrs Jack,' corrects Bike.

'Mrs Jack told him to,' says Sass, 'but Jack brought it. Didn't he, Mum? Jack brought it.'

The mother nods, smiles.

'See,' says Sass, leering at her brother.

'See, see,' mimics Bike, and pulls out an imaginary pair of binoculars which he waves around the room.

'Mongrel,' says Sass. 'Don't listen to my mongrel brother, Mr Martin David. He can't help it. He's adopted.'

'Liar.' Bike turns to his mother for reassurance.

She pats him on the shoulder, saying, 'Oh, she's being silly.'

Bike sits, repeating the word 'silly' under his breath.

The fresh food is delicious, the salad succulent. M has a second serving of everything.

'How was your trip?' the woman asks, tries again.

'No problems, no problems.'

'Is it cold up?'

'No, not too bad.'

'Oh, that's right, you don't feel the cold.' She smiles and pushes a piece of chicken to the side of her plate.

'Not much, not really.'

'Snow?'

'Not this time.'

'How long then, do you think, till snow?'

'Hard to say, hard to pick it. Who can tell?'

'Now, now,' she says, with the same little smile on her red, red lips, 'you always know, darling. Doesn't he, kids? He always knows.'

They eat. Soon the woman pipes up again.

'Are you sure you're not cold?'

'I'm fine, thank you. Fine, really.'

'Oh.' She smiles, puts down her fork and pulls her jumper to her chest.

'He's fine, Mum,' says Sass. 'Aren't you.'

He nods.

'We missed you,' says the woman. 'I missed you.'

Now he sees it: she is drug-addled and confused.

'Tell us what you saw,' says Sass.

'Yeah, yeah, what did you see? What's up there?' Bike is excited. He bangs his fork on the table.

'Shut up, idiot!' snaps Sass. 'Go on,' she says, 'did you catch any devils?'

'One or two,' he says, 'but I let them go.'

Sass is impressed. But she wants to know more.

'Did you catch anything else? You know? Anything . . . ?'

''Fraid not. Devils is what I was after, and devils is what I got.'

'You know, but, anything else? Any-thing.' She opens her eyes wide and puts one finger on the tip of her nose as if to say, 'You can tell me, don't worry about them.'

'Well,' he says, and the girl almost stops breathing. 'Well, I caught a water bottle.'

She waits. Her father's water bottle?

'A blue one,' he continues.

In the photo the missing man had a blue water bottle sticking out of one pocket.

'A blue one . . .' says Sass. 'And, go on, yeah, go on.'

'Nothing else, nothing.'

After a few minutes she asks, 'Can I see it?'

'Well no, sorry, I couldn't fit it in my pack.'

'But – why not?' She looks as if she wants to cry; a tremor passes through her lower lip.

'Because I couldn't fit it.'

She stares at him, stares into his bones. She sits and stares and he realises he has made a mistake. The girl is no fool, she saw him packing the bloody hearts and livers, and once he'd taken them out he would, on any miser's calculations, have ample room in his pack. But does a girl really know these things? She is thinking something, yes, but what?

'I've got a water bottle,' says Bike proudly and he seems taken aback when his sister lets him speak. 'Two hundred million of them.' And still his sister is quiet.

M sleeps well and rises the next day, as usual, before the rest of the household. He decides to go into town again, to enquire after renting a room at the pub. At Sid's Supermarket he stocks up on fresh vegetables, and the happy butcher, he is surprised to discover, is in a bad mood.

He orders a steak at the pub and, when he is finished, goes over to pay at the bar. The publican takes his money.

'About rooms,' says M, pocketing his change, 'how much to rent a room?'

'No vacancies,' says the publican.

No vacancies?

'What do you mean?' asks M.

'Like I said, mate, no vacancies.'

Not possible.

'Anyone leaving?'

'All regulars, mate, live-ins.' The publican looks around the room. The drinkers are alert and territorial: now they have something to listen to.

'I'll pay double.'

'Pay me triple if you want, mate, same difference.'

And with that the publican closes the till and retires to the kitchen.

'Eh, you,' beckons a drinker further down the bar. 'You want a room?'

Ah, an opportunity. M goes to sweet-talk the geezer.

'Yeah, mate. I need a room.'

'Yeah?'

'Yeah.'

'Yeah, well,' the old man breaks into a wheezy pink-faced laugh, 'you can't have one!' This causes considerable mirth amongst the drinkers; they grin and sink their beers.

One drinker, younger than the others, wearing a flannelette shirt and sturdy canvas pants, calls him over:

'You, come here, mate. Over here, yeah. Pull up a pew.'

M stands.

'You're staying out at the Armstrong place, yeah? We heard about you.'

M stands.

'From where?' He looks across the room for confirmation. 'From the mainland aren't ya, some university, eh? You don't look like one, but.'

The drinking men are clearly aroused.

M says, 'I'll pay double for your room.'

'Would ya? Just one thing, mate. We don't take greenie cunts round here. So unless you want to join your mate Jarrah Fucking Armstrong, fuck off.'

'Fuck off!' The old man finds this hysterically funny and

launches into a coughing fit. Another drinker starts crooning 'Are You Lonesome Tonight?' ... he croons and stares, makes himself ugly. Others start banging the bottom of their glasses against the table-tops. M is tempted to smack his fist into the face of the smirking man before him, but he holds himself back. Now is a time for patience; he is a professional and he will not do anything to jeopardise the hunt. Yes, that's right, patience, his temper cools, be patient.

Back at the house any fears M once had about the girl's persuasions are confirmed. It is not obvious at first, but he notices it: his pack is not exactly as he had left it; it has moved about thirty centimetres towards his bed. He carries out an inspection. Nothing is missing, but it is patent someone has been carefully through his belongings. His rifle is still locked in its case. I will not confront her, he thinks, it is enough that I know.

Late at night, very late, when he is compelled to take a piss, he hears a voice in Sleeping Beauty's chamber. No, it's not the woman, but the prying daughter. Her voice slips and slides, borders on a whisper. He stands outside and strains to listen ...

'... And Bike's OK, but, he's OK. I think. You know, he's a dumb idiot who doesn't know anything. But don't tell him I told you that or he'd kill me. So anyway, that's good, isn't it. That's good ...

'... Promise you won't get mad? Promise cross your heart and stick a needle in your eye? OK then, I'll tell you ... Mr Martin David said he found Dad's water bottle, you know, the blue one. The one we gave him for Christmas

64

last year, and he said it was the best present he ever had, you know, the shiny blue one. Well, Mr Martin David said he found it. So, that's good, isn't it . . .

'. . . A liar, capital L-I-A-R. Because I went into his room, even though you told me not to. But I had to, because of the water bottle. That's OK, isn't it? . . . But it wasn't there . . . He's not nice, is he? Not really . . . OK Mum, don't you worry about it, it'll be OK, I promise . . . OK then . . . Night, Mum . . . Nighty-night . . .'

He hears the girl get up off the bed, kiss her silent mother goodnight. Then he disappears back to bed.

Over the next two days the woman does not leave her room. M, meanwhile, is surprised by the girl's behaviour: she is kinder to him than he would have expected. But kind, he thinks, is not quite right. She is not being kind but simply 'not unkind'. When she can, it is clear she chooses to avoid him. For a novice in these matters of duplicity, he wants to say, you're doing very well.

⬤

Upon his return to the plateau he discovers every shrub and rock and tarn has abandoned the glorious sun and retreated into low-lying cloud. He takes a new route, planning to set new traps and snares before swinging back around to check his earlier lines. The old-timers used to say a thylacine wouldn't go near a snare unless it was at least a week old, and M sees no reason why his tiger shouldn't be equally wary. Perhaps more so. But, he reminds himself as he trudges forward one step at a time, who really knows? Other tiger-men claimed to have snared sixteen tigers in a day. Ha! The heydays ... And besides, what good is history when he is not seeking all tigers, but one tiger: the last one.

Is she wary, he wonders, trained in the elusive arts by a furtive parent, or simply lucky? Or unlucky. And after years of inbreeding does she bear any behavioural resemblance to her forebears? Or is making it through each day a sickly exercise done with the same decrepit sense of purpose as a coma victim in a nursing home? Does she even have the energy to kill, or has she — like that zoo-bound handful before her — descended to picking at carrion? Is her striped and honeyed coat short and dense like that of a Doberman's, or has it fallen to maggot-ridden mange?

This ignoble image of his prey discourages M and he immediately sets about to rectify it: Yes, there is virtue in being a survivor. The last tiger must be wary, she must be strong, she must be crafty and ruthless and wise. And if the mutation has endowed her with any new qualities, they must be qualities which enhance, not detract from, the inescapable drive to survive. Otherwise she would not be alive, otherwise the winter would have claimed her. And no, she does not spend her days in a sickly fashion, rather she greets each day as a new opportunity to track the scent of a mate. That is what propels her day after day across the plateau: immortality.

And while he is fortifying the thylacine, the natural man's eye catches a tiny flash of red between two rocks.

He dumps his pack and goes to investigate. What is it? A stoic's baby? Or – what? Surely not a remnant of the missing man? Perhaps now he'll have something to return to the girl. He hopes so.

Yes, he hopes so.

What he finds is a bandanna. Did the missing man wear a bandanna? He didn't seem the jaunty type, but again, who's to know? M marks the spot on his photograph and pockets the piece of cloth. He explores the surrounding area and soon finds his answer: two muddy sets of boot-prints. Not the missing man but a couple of bushwalkers, perhaps rangers. From the size and depth of the prints – one set large and deep, the other shallow, narrow and short – he guesses a man and woman have walked this way some time in the last two dry days since rain. They are headed, he determines, along the open pass, bearing a steady ninety degrees away from his route. He stands and fingers the bandanna, thinks a while: They are not walking my way and so they will not disturb me. There is nothing I can do. Carry on as planned.

He works hard, rejuvenated after his last sojourn. By dusk he has set one snare and one trap. The white cloud has not lifted, and visibility across an open stretch of pineapple-grass bog is poor. After eating – fresh mung beans grown that day in a plastic jar strapped to his pack – he takes up a position and prepares to sit. As a concession to his new neighbours he decides not to use his head-torch. The night is cold, the cloud-bank damp. He sits downwind and waits. A brush-tailed possum wanders close, and with his rifle scope he traces its outline, and then proceeds to dissect it, as he would if he were skinning it: tailbone to the neck, carefully bypassing the anus; up alongside the penis, avoiding the bladder tube; skilfully negotiating his way through the gut area towards the ribs; then dropping back down behind each rear leg; next the front legs and, finally, a necklace. Ready to peel. Like a piece of fruit. He remembers the first time he ever skinned a rabbit; how he botched the job, piercing the gut with the point of his knife. The stink! But he'd kept going, he'd peeled it, even though it took all his strength to turn the skinny thing inside out. It was so purple and scrawny, he couldn't believe it. If I hadn't been a country boy, he wonders, would I ever have been able to do it?

Some hours later he hears a scuffle in the scrub where his trap is set. He gets up and slowly makes his way over. Another wallaby. This one he kills by quickly slashing its throat, again deferring to his neighbours. He wouldn't want to wake them with the resounding crack of his rifle. The wallaby shudders, falls quiet. M decides to go ahead and skin the creature: a bit of practice, keep his hand in, give him something to do. He has no trouble, pausing only at the ribs where the pearly skin adheres strongly to the flesh and bones: jab and lift, jab and lift. Soon the job is done. He cuts the thin membrane along the ribs and then, with a better view, separates the intestines from the gut membrane. This is delicate work. He dislodges the bladder tube from the pelvis and ties it in a knot to prevent any urine escaping. Don't you piss on me, he says under his breath, don't you piss on me ... With one hand he reaches in and pulls out a tumble of blue and pink intestines, each covered in a filigree of white fat. Then the red-black liver. The fatty kidneys are wedged down the back. Finished, he inspects the meat and decides that it is too watery and bruised to eat, but good enough for bait. He hacks through joints, bundles the disarticulated pieces and viscera back into the skin and carries the thing, less skull and paws, back to his little tent. It will stink, he knows, but it is late and he is tired and doesn't really care.

In the morning he scrubs the gore off his hands and forearms and knife, using a small miry tarn as a washbasin and a handful of tea-tree as his scrubbing brush. Ah, clean. Clean as a baby's bottom. That's what his girlfriend – his only girlfriend – used to say as she dallied around the kitchen with her tea-towel. He'd found it funny for some unknown reason, the way people will laugh themselves stupid over a particularly dumb joke ... Clean as a baby's bottom ... But it wasn't funny, and this memory gives rise to faint nausea, it wasn't funny when she got pregnant, the two of them at the Defence Academy, and he'd had to borrow money to pay for the abortion ... After all these years he's surprised he still remembers.

Five days later, when he is done setting his new runs, he collects some repair wire he has stashed and heads out to his old lines. There he finds a frozen menagerie: pademelons, wallabies (again, more wallabies), devils, native cats, two barred bandicoots, a feral cat, a shiny black currawong and, in one trap, a squat young wombat. The wombat is still alive, and M shoots it in the head. He cleans the trap in some water, thinking: I am patient and I still have time.

As he had expected, the traps prove to be more successful than the snares. On the first three runs checked he finds that most of the traps have been sprung, and few of these are empty. One trap, he sees, has been sprung by a fallen branch. The others he puts down to a little cunning: the bait is always gone. It is possible, he knows, that the tiger has sniffed out the bait and in wisdom reincarnate teased the trigger, standing back as the deathly jaws rose up out of the earth to snatch at – nothing. If I were superstitious, he fancies, I might suspect a ghost tiger had roamed nearby. But he is not that way inclined, and so around every trap and snare he sets about looking for prints or droppings: any tangible hint of the tiger's presence. When I have a fix on you, he thinks, I promise I won't let go.

He has almost finished this circuit when he comes across another set of boot-prints. The prints are all about one of his limp snares and he recognises them immediately: pandemonium. Inspecting the wire loop, he sees that it has been severed with something sharp, like a knife. The sapling, he can't help but notice, has been wrenched in two and laid on the dun pad in the form of a cross. A human hex. Under the cross is a dirty piece of paper weighted down with a small rock. In heavy lead pencil someone has scrawled 'FUCK YOU'. Christ! He hopes it was a bushwalker, not a ranger. He hopes it was a tourist. But what is hope? Hope is nothing. And – think now, think straight, breathe – what can he can do? Look around,

70

take counsel. The dwarf beech knows, the dolerite knows: there is nothing to do but be what he is, to tend his runs and sit at night. He will need to be careful. This latest is a passing storm, a turn of the wheel, a blink of an eye. So be it. He will carry on.

M checks the remaining traps and snares in the run. None of them, to his great relief, seem to have been spotted. If they were rangers, he thinks, they would have looked. He allows himself to relax a little. The hunt will not be compromised; it is probable that the danger is past.

Later that night, during the long hours, his mind turns to the collapsed snare and the broken sapling. Yes, he confesses to the chill wind, he cannot deny the fact: it bothers him that he and the tiger are no longer alone.

In the six weeks that have passed since M's unfortunate mention of the water bottle there has grown between the girl and himself a strange intimacy, the kind of wary intimacy to be found amongst old friends who have in the past betrayed one another. It began, he supposes, when he brought her the bandanna and the small half-moon purse he stitched together from wallaby skin. The bandanna, as he suspected, did not belong to her father, but she seemed pleased that he had thought to bring it down. And when he had handed her the purse she had let loose a little smile, and said by way of girlish forgiveness, 'What is it? . . . It's nice.'

71

From then on the girl had talked to him on his rest days, even going to a little trouble to help him out. The boy, too, as ever, seemed to like him. And the Sleeping Beauty? She continued to do what she did best: sleep and dream and hope for the worst to pass. According to the children, Mrs Mindy visited on occasion, always bringing food and sitting beside her becalmed charge. She telephoned too, asking for Sass, and he noticed that every time she did the girl's spirits lifted. He is not surprised, then, when one morning after one of these calls, the girl takes him by the hand and invites him, or rather, leads him, to the vegetable garden. The boy follows.

'Carrots grow here,' says Sass, pointing to the patch of garden where Bike is trailing his hands through neat rows of leafy green stalks. 'Do you know about carrots?'

Does he know about carrots?

'Do you know when they're big enough to pick?' she asks, hopes, hungry.

Oh. 'They're big enough,' he says and disengages, turns back to the house.

That night M cooks up the carrots and some rice, adding a little fish he bought the day before in town. Because Bike insists on watching, M offers to let him help, even shows him the proper way to slice the carrots, on an angle so they catch more heat. He enjoys this cooking, the pleasure of hot food. In fact, on his trips up the plateau it's true that he almost looks forward to hovering over the steaming stove. So involved are the two men in their cooking that the sight of Lucy Armstrong, wearing a clean blue dress, with her hair neatly pulled back, takes them by surprise.

'What's this?' she asks pleasantly.

Bike drops his knife on the table and runs to hug his mother's waist.

'Dinner,' says Sass, who has followed her mother into the kitchen.

'Smells delicious,' says the woman. 'Jamie, come and help me set the table.'

'My new name's Bike,' he mumbles into the soft folds of her dress.

'Bike, eh? Bike. I suppose that's not too bad. Alright then, Bike, let's go. And you, Katie, have you got a new name too?'

'Sass,' she replies. 'From Sassafras.'

'That's pretty. What about me, do I get one?'

'You're Mum,' says Bike.

Sass is quiet.

Throughout the meal Sass scrutinises her mother, scarcely talks. When M makes conversation about the vegetable patch (yes, the vegetable patch — it has come to this), Sass shoots him a fierce look: Be quiet. Don't trust her, the sleepwalker. The woman, meanwhile, eats and talks:

'So, Martin, how is the study going? Those devils giving you trouble?'

'You know what they're like, but no, not much trouble. I'm getting what I need.'

'My husband, you know, worked on the plateau . . .' She pauses, starts again. 'We've only been down here two years.'

73

'Two years, really?'

'And what was your department again, zoology?'

'Yes, zoology.'

'You've read Jarrah's book, then?'

'Top of my list – sorry, that's embarrassing.'

'*Bioethics for Another Millennium* – my title; you haven't read it?'

'That's right.'

'Not for your course?'

'No, not yet.'

She thinks a while. 'Jamie, go and get Dad's book to show Mr David.'

Bike slaps down his fork and leaves the table.

'What do they teach in zoology these days, then?'

'Well, it hasn't really changed much in the last ten years. A little, perhaps.'

Bike comes back empty-handed. 'Couldn't find it,' he says, sits down and starts to eat.

'I'll find it later,' promises Lucy. 'Miss Sassafras,' she says, turning to her daughter and smiling brightly, 'isn't this dinner delicious?'

'So?'

The mother manages another smile.

Sass sticks out her lower lip, plays with her fish.

'I have an announcement,' says Lucy.

They wait.

'Tomorrow you two are going back to school.'

'Erghhh,' groans Bike, clutching his stomach as if he's been hit by a bullet.

'But –' protests Sass. 'But why? We don't have to, you can't make us.'

'Yes I can. Mrs Mindy is coming to collect you at eight o'clock sharp.'

'Mrs Mindeee . . .' Bike groans again.

Sass says nothing.

When the meal is over the children vanish into their bedroom and M is left alone with the sleepwalker. Her eyes, he notices, have thinned their glaze. Does she expect me to say something? he wonders. What? Anything? But as soon as the children are out of earshot, she is the one to break the awkward silence:

'I've stopped taking my pills.'

Oh. He nods: I understand. But he doesn't understand. He can only guess, and he guesses her somnambular search is over, called off. Now, he guesses, she wants her life back.

And so it goes on. M returns to the plateau and the children return to school. He carries out his hunt: twelve days up, two days down. Twelve days up, two days down. Continual rain, merciless rain, and still he searches, twelve days up, two days down. But nowhere, nowhere, the tiger. Time grows fat in the bottom of the hourglass; never before has he been away so long on a job.

Inside the bluestone house subtle changes are taking place, and he observes these on his two-day visits with his naturalist's eye. The woman no longer keeps to her bed –

75

instead, she has turned her attentions to the house itself, cleaning and prettying, filling vases with fresh flowers. At night she cooks. Her own appearance begins to improve, her lips lose their blood-drained pallor, her shoulders roll back and her head stands high. She wears clean clothes. When he is around she takes care of his needs, making sure he is warm and well fed. On his advice she takes trips to town to buy supplies. She starts to talk, to make general conversation. He finds this does not annoy him as he thought it might: she is pleasant and good-humoured, and while she likes to talk, she does not like to talk too much. He wonders when – and if – she will get close enough to kiss him. But she is not, he sees, entirely drug-free, not always consistent. The occasional haze, a relaxed indifference, is difficult to detect – and he imagines that more than once he must have been fooled. And the young? Naturally they have been affected by their mother's revival. The girl, he sees, has grown quiet, as if her own energy had been depleted and turned to others' ends. She hibernates. And the boy – the boy follows the strongest current. He stays by his mother's side and, on those days when she is distracted, he – knowing no shame – returns to, and is comforted by, his sister. Of course, M does not know what goes on when he is away, whether the mother and daughter come to blows, whether the boy ever spirits himself away, whether the three of them laugh or cry, but he makes his hypotheses on the information available and takes these with him to the plateau to contemplate when everything else has failed to interest him.

He is drinking hot tea one evening when he spies, stuck to the refrigerator, a drawing. Not any drawing: a thylacine. The animal is drawn in brown texta, and stands side on, with one pointy ear and a wide-open jaw filled with blue triangles, or teeth. The body is in outline only, and the two legs nearest the viewer form part of this outline, as does an upright tail, while the far legs hang from the tiger's belly like a pair of teats. Running down the back of the tiger are thick black stripes. To the right of the floating creature is a floating fire, a red and orange scribble above a tangle of black sticks: a cave drawing. In the bottom right corner of the drawing is the word 'James', with the 's' drawn the wrong way around.

'That's a good drawing, Bike,' says M. 'What is it?'

'Tiger, idiot-brain,' Bike replies, and continues colouring in the faces in his mother's magazine.

'A tiger? Really? What kind of tiger? Indian tiger?'

'Tasmanian tiger.'

'Oh, I see, a Tasmanian tiger.'

'Yep.'

'So how come you did a picture of a Tasmanian tiger and not an Indian tiger?'

'Because,' says Bike, 'the teacher said we had to. She told us the story about the tiger and how he got his stripes and said we had to draw it. Mine was the best. True.'

'His stripes – how did he get his stripes?'

'From the fire, you know.'

'I'm an idiot-brain, can you tell me?'

Bike rolls his eyes.

'OK, well, once there was a spirit called *palanna* or something and a giant kangaroo jumped on him and then a baby tiger pup came along and said don't worry *palanna* or whatever I'll save you and he bit the kangaroo in the neck and wouldn't let go and the kangaroo jumped around but the pup still wouldn't let go and then the kangaroo fell down dead and *palanna* went home and saw his parents and then they had a fire and *palanna* got some of the blood from the fight with the kangaroo and stuck his hand in the fire and got out the grey ash and mixed it together and painted the stripes on the tiger's back so he could show everyone how brave he was. OK? Got it?'

'Good story,' says M.

'Dumb story. I hate school.'

M waits a minute or two, watches the boy colour in.

'You know they don't exist,' he says, drinks his tea.

'What?' Bike keeps his head down, lips pursed in concentration.

'Tasmanian tigers.'

'Do so.'

'Do not.'

'Do so.'

'I don't think so.'

'Do too. I know.'

'How do you know?'

'Because I know, because my dad saw one.'

M stops. Starts again.

'I bet he didn't, really.'

'He did so.' And now Bike looks up, angrily, from his

work. 'He did so see one. It was up on the plateau. He saw it good.'

'Did he really?' M keeps his voice soft, cajoling.

'Last summer. It's a big secret. Don't tell anyone.' He's back colouring in again. 'My dad saw it.'

'Did you tell your teacher?'

Now Bike looks up again. 'It's top secret.'

Before he leaves once more, M finds the mother alone in the chook-pen. When she sees him coming she smiles, and this gives him confidence. Hers is the generous type of smile that fills a whole face.

'Good morning,' she says.

'Good morning.'

'So, off again?'

'Just about.'

'Back in twelve, by six?'

'Back in twelve.'

She cradles the basket of eggs under one arm and leans with the other against the jamb of the wooden gate.

'I was thinking,' she begins, 'about next week, well, almost two weeks really. You see, there's going to be a festival. Have you heard, a folk festival?'

Her voice is a little sharp, high. He waits, smiles.

'So, if you wanted, we could maybe go together. For a few hours, if you wanted.'

'Sounds alright.'

'Oh, does it? Good. Good. Thanks. Oh that's good . . . I

should get out a bit more, you know.'

Ever the gentleman, he changes the topic.

'By the way,' he says, 'I like Bike's picture on the fridge.'

'Oh, that.' She looks away, just a little.

'Tasmanian tiger, is it?'

'So he says.'

Her grip on the basket is so tight the tops of her knuckles show white.

'They're everywhere,' he jokes.

She smiles, but this time it's a stillborn smile. Now he has seen enough.

'Alright then, I'm off, see you later.'

'OK, good, see you later. Take care.'

Take care – she says it like she means it.

———

If it had not occurred to him before, he realises it now as once again the plateau opens out before him: the boy's drawing has brought him comfort. Yes, comfort. Today he is the spy who, after months of inactivity in a steamy port town full of manic gamblers and corrupt sweating officials, is beginning to think he has been abandoned (ah, too well he knows this kind of town), and who, on reading the morning newspapers, unexpectedly catches sight of a coded message and knows he is not alone. He is, M concedes, exaggerating – but why not? It's only himself he is fooling, buoying. Who else is there? The sky-flecked plateau, for one, is impervious. If this is what's called clutching at

80

straws, then today the straws are firmly anchored to that higher, better part of him that so rarely sees the light of day. Perhaps, he thinks as he weaves through the yellow-bush, this is what it is like to be truly happy ... But he does not dare dwell too long on these matters, and instead enjoys his light step and the easy swing of his arms.

And to his pleasant surprise this feeling of comfort survives the day: survives a slip in the creek which leaves him with a mulberry-blue bruise on one shin; survives a light lunch of cheese and scroggin; survives endless muddy patches devoid of tiger prints; survives the discovery of a missing trap. The missing trap puzzles him and, while he cannot be sure, he decides it is most likely that a ferocious devil, summoning the powers of good and evil, has managed to rip the retaining spike out of the ground. They were furious snorting grunting things, those devils, and never gave up without a fight. Not like the tiger. When the tiger was trapped it let itself go. Some trappers said they died of shock, but other sensitive souls preferred the ancient and redeeming thought that the tiger chose its time to die, the trapper being a mere conduit. Others again, the noble men, thought the tiger was a noble beast who refused to suffer the indignity of capture. So in 1936, when the Johnson boy led a tiger down the escarpment and chained it up at his father's dairy farm, such men were not the least surprised to learn that overnight the tiger had jumped the fence, thereby hanging itself. Of these spectral theories M has no favourite: he is happiest to wait and see.

By dusk this strange but welcome feeling has not

evaporated. He drops his pack at the top of a steep ridge, and settles with his rifle on a promontory of rock overlooking a stretch of button-grass. In the half-light the clouds blush violently, sober up; a sharp-beaked currawong calls to a friend. M sits. He hears the thud-thud of a wallaby passing not far behind him, but does not turn to look. He lets an inch-man trail over his mountainous boot. The scent of lemon boronia is ushered by on a light breeze. M continues to sit. Darkness falls; the stars take their infinite curtain-call. He sits and feels his body grow light, disappear, so now there is no skin between himself and the plateau. He expands. The huge deep ground he is sitting on is holding him up, but soon there is no such thing as up: he is nowhere, everywhere. When he breathes he can sense the air cool as it flows over the moisture in his nostrils, his belly swells, then the same air, now a little warmer, flows out again. This is what he focuses on: the air in and the air out, and in time he is nothing but something through which air passes, just as it passes through the shivering treetops below him, over stones, slips through blades of grass. The black night grows cold, and still he sits.

In the morning he lies in his sleeping bag and listens to the rain patter against his tent. The comfort has changed, yes, but has not left him. He dresses and eats, breaks camp. Throughout the day he checks his runs and sets new snares. The rain thins, stops, the clouds dissipate and drift. He cuts carcasses from his traps and drags them up and down the pad, marking their scent. Again, the sky colours pink and mauve, and again he prepares to sit.

On the morning of the twelfth day, just as he is headed back toward the escarpment, he finds a wallaby corpse with its throat ripped red-raw. On closer inspection he sees the heart, lungs, kidneys and liver have been consumed, along with some meat from the inside of the ham. Nothing else has been touched. There are none of the usual tell-tale signs of a struggle. And when the Naturalist gently lays his wet hand on the animal he feels the faintest warmth. A fresh kill, displaying all the characteristics of a tiger kill. He refuses to be excited, thinking only: This rain will have washed away any prints. The first thing he does is mark his position clearly on his photograph. Then he searches his surrounds. He follows a nearby pad, stopping when it fractures into a creek. Nothing. He returns to the site of the kill and picks another path to follow; this one climbs a small snow gum studded rise, immediately dropping down the other side to linger along the edge of a marshy stretch of cord rush. M has been following this route for an hour, checking for possible rest spots along the way, when he finds a dry patch of flattened tussock grass below two interlocking slabs of dolerite. He presses his hand onto the grass to feel for heat and thinks he feels some. Any animal could have stopped here for some respite from the beating rain, it's true, but M takes out his photograph and marks it with a tiny circle.

Now I have you.

Looking at his watch he sees he will have to hurry if he wants to be back before dark: the alarm must not be raised. So, turning from the dolerite, he takes a bearing and strides off into the new world, electrified and blood aflame.

***

She is happy to see him. At the sound of his car she has come out of the house to wait on the lawn, with one hand deep in her skirt pocket and the other waving – feebly, it seems – in greeting. She's smiling that big smile. He manages to twinkle the fingers of one hand in response, thinking: What's this? A welcoming committee? At the dinner table that night he realises something about the woman is different, and then he notices – her hair. She's dyed her hair a light shade of red, run a rinse through it. It might even be a little shorter than before.

'Haircut?' he asks.

'Oh that, I got it yesterday.'

'Looks good.'

'Thanks.'

'Where are the children?'

She brings out an earthenware pot wrapped in a tea-towel.

'They've already eaten,' she says, smiles, sits down, sighs, takes the lid off the pot and inhales deeply. 'Lentil casserole.'

She's also prepared a green salad. A mound of olives rests in a leaf-shaped green pottery bowl.

'A glass of wine?' she suggests.

'Just a drop.'

He eats quickly and lets her do most, if not all, of the

talking. He learns a lot, more than he needs to know: she is a Capricorn; she studied law but dropped out in her final year; she took time out, almost three years, to travel through India and Nepal. This evening she loves to talk.

'My father,' she says, 'was happy to hear I was moving to Tasmania. "Safe from nuclear fall-out," he said – he thought we'd be safe at the far end of the earth . . .'

She pauses and M sees she can't escape her missing husband, and he also sees she is aware that he has noticed. Now he is awkward – what should he say?

'I'm sorry,' says M, 'about your husband.' Will that do?

She hesitates. 'That's alright,' she replies, 'that's fine . . . really, I mean, it's OK.' She is lying, he knows it. But what else can she be expected to reply? That things will never be alright, never fine. That every day she remembers what she has lost, which is not disturbing because she resents losing her love, but rather because she no longer knows which is more important – her memories past or her experience in the present. The difference between the two is papery-thin.

She goes to the bathroom. While she is gone he imagines what it would be like to fuck her, what kind of cunt she has. He imagines what she'd look like undoing her bra. Enough! He could do it, he could have a few drinks and persuade her, but he won't. He can resist the warm tidal pull, at least – and this is more palatable – he will resist it until the job is over. He chews his food: I am a professional, I have patience. Patience is a virtue. This self-hypnosis does the trick, so that by the time she returns he has nearly

85

forgotten (nearly but not quite) his lustful fantasies. They eat quickly, her talking experiment has been doused. As soon as he is finished he excuses himself.

'Goodnight,' he says.

She sits there flickering in the candlelight. 'Goodnight.'

That night in bed he has an erection, and two deft minutes later it is dismantled.

At breakfast the next day Sass is wearing the silver and purple catsuit he'd first seen her in, and Bike his glittering silver cape. Today they are fidgeting more than usual, as if everything they touched – chairs, cutlery, table-top – was studded with uncomfortable brass bumps or was painfully hot.

'When are we going? When are we going?' begs Bike.

'You two are full of beans,' says Lucy. 'After you've finished your eggs and cleaned your hands and I've straightened up.'

She turns to M.

'The folk festival starts today. Are you still coming?'

'Yabba yabba!' says Bike.

A windowful of golden morning light falls over her shoulders, through her fine red hair.

'Not today, sorry. I've got a lot of paperwork to get through.' He slices a piece of his fried egg and pushes it against the buttery toast. 'I'll be going up again tomorrow.'

'Oh well, kids, not to worry ... Another time, eh.'

'When?' asks Sass, deliberately.

The mother takes a sip of tea.

He is in his room studying his photographs and checking his equipment when he hears Lucy calling from the kitchen: 'Jamie! Katie! Time to go!'

She calls out the back door: 'Time to go! Kids! Time to go!'

No response. Curious, he thinks, resumes his examination of the rifle.

Out the front he hears her yelling: 'Jamieee! Katieee!'

There's a knock on his door, and he shoves the rifle under a heap of his clothes, saying: 'Come in.'

She sticks her head in. 'Sorry to disturb you, have you seen the little monsters?'

'Not since breakfast.'

'Thanks.'

He hears the persistent toot tooooooot toooooot of a car horn.

Half an hour later the woman knocks on his door again. Her skin, he notices, is drained of colour.

'Sorry,' she says, 'it's the kids. Maybe if you tried . . .'

What can he say? 'No problem.

'Sass! Bike! Your mother's ready!'

'Game's over now, kids! We're going! Katie! Jamie! Right now! . . . Right now! I mean it!'

No luck. Her breath quickens, she runs her hand through her hair. A change has come over her, an animal who has sniffed a predator on the wind. There is nothing he can do.

'We'll find them,' he says, smiles.

But the woman looks at him in horror. She looks at him and he can see what she does not need to say: You're lying, you're lying, they're missing, everyone's always lying. She closes her eyes for a long time, out there in the sunny paddock by the three wrecked cars. The ragwort, he sees, is pushing up through rusty holes in the floor of one car: the car is in flower. Then the woman begins to cry, but the tears don't flow freely, and she makes the same ungodly noises he imagines she would make if she were being strangled. She hides her face in her hands. They return to the house, his hand in the warm small of her back. Then he hears it — yes, he can definitely hear it — coming from her bedroom, a muffled giggle, a high-pitched squeal.

With Lucy in tow he goes to the bedroom and pushes the door open wide, calling: 'Found you!' Suddenly the mound of blankets and doonas at the foot of the bed comes alive, erupts. The children emerge red-faced and sweaty, hair amuck. Both can hardly stop giggling. Oh! The relief! So hot and sticky down there!

The woman marches over and slaps Sass in the face. Then she grabs both her children and pulls them to her chest, squashes them tight against her. Sass, he sees, is on the verge of tears.

'Oh God,' moans the woman, 'don't ever do that again. Never. So worried, I was so ... worried.' She rocks the children back and forth. Bike is confused and starts to cry. Sass doesn't cry. One side of her face is buried in her mother's chest, and with her free shiny eye she stares at M, resolute in her hopelessness: And you, what do you think you're looking at? He walks away.

The mother calls off the excursion and takes to her bed. Dinnertime comes and goes without ceremony. The children

88

stay in their room. He fixes himself some food. Still the woman finds toxic salvation in her soft warm bed. And when he leaves in the early rose-pink hours of the morning neither she nor the children have stirred.

———

He knows exactly where to go. The site of the kill and the patch of flattened grass have grounded him, and though he has only two fixed points, perhaps only one, he is as certain as a mathematician poised to draw a straight line. But first he must collect his traps which are hidden in areas now of little use to him: from what he knows, it is unlikely that the tiger will pass their way. They can be reset, he reminds himself, and every trap must count.

Soon enough he is back, kneeling down between the two interlocking dolerite slabs, raking his sensitive hands through the grass and dirt.

Come and rest here now, he thinks. Come and rest.

He carries on. He passes through the cool dark avenues of a pencil-pine forest, feels the soft fragrant needle carpet beneath his feet. In here, he thinks, one could sleep. He sets a run of four traps and, because the pines all look the same, even to his natural-eye, he tags some nearby branches. Out of the forest he follows a pad that runs, speeds, through the tussock grass until it comes to a white sandy cove and drowns itself in a lake. The lake is braceleted with dark pines, and rising beyond them is a thin and austere dolerite ridge, a giant semi-circular wall. The wind, he sees, has stirred up the lake, made little white-tipped ripples. The sky, too, is whitening. Tonight it will be cold.

As he walks he spies a snow-daisy to one side of the pad. One little flower – as if someone had dropped it on their way through. The flower reminds him of women, women in general, because women and flowers, for some reason, and he realises he doesn't know what reason, are one and the same thing. And this thinking of women, and flowers, and this walking with a feeling of comfort and certainty, emboldens in him a memory often neglected: that feeling of romance. Yes, he is romancing his prey. This thought rankles him a little, because at heart he knows he is only hunting, but for entertainment's sake he lets it run. Yes, he is in the early days, those first few heady days of romance, when he has already bedded the girl, whispered in her ear, sent her roses, whispered her mouth is a rose, that she is filled with roses, roses beneath her skin, a rose between her legs blah blah (here a tickle as he whispers). He has confessed his jealousy, watched her soften before him, watched her soften but not quite give herself over. And that is what he is after: he wants to see her give herself up. He wants to be there when she tiptoes across the line. But no, enough, he stops himself. This nostalgia for seduction is seductive itself. And it's delusory. The animal is no woman. He will not win it over with sweet words, wine and roses. Look around, there are no roses here.

The night is cold, the coldest yet. M is tempted to light a fire but desists: a fire can be smelt miles away. He chews beef jerky and watches over black lacquered tarns; his beanie is pulled down low and his Polartech collar rides high around his cheeks. From where he is camped he can see the top of the dolerite wall running dark against the dark starless sky. He waits until the appointed hour and then sleeps. Lying there on the hard ground inside his tent he performs his favourite trick: he changes shape, swallows the beast. The eyes in his head are no longer his own, short thick fur runs along the back of his neck, and his spine grows thick and strong, right out of his back, out into a long stiff tail. He hangs his body off this strong spine, hollows out his belly, shrinks his gangly limbs. His arm is bent at the elbow, and a paw, not a hand, rests against his bony convex chest. He sleeps and hopes to dream.

In the cold raw morning M is once again himself. After checking his maps he heads north-east. He has not been gone long, not even three hours, before he jumps down a rock ledge and swings around to catch – what! – a stick – slipping under his cap, right into the corner of his eye. Fuck! Fuck it. He blinks, startled, the eye begins to smart. He offloads his pack and rinses the eye in clean cold water, relieved to find it is not bleeding. It could have been worse, he thinks. By midday the eye has swollen so that it becomes an effort to keep it open. He looks for eyebright, a tiny flowering herb he has seen before, and which he knows would make a good eye-wash: not to be found. The skin below his eyebrow balloons out to meet his eyelashes. He tries not to touch it. He decides to cut the day short, to walk until he reaches the next suitable vantage point and go no further. The swollen eye undermines his certainty: he watches his step.

And almost as if in condolence, or by way of encouragement and reassurance, it is on this day that he sees the tiger has left him a print: the tiger, or maybe the plateau. Is it really? Could it be? Stop, take a good look. There it is in a muddy patch, one of the thousands of muddy patches he has inspected, yes, a wallaby spoor, and what looks like the forefoot of a thylacine. The print is about five centimetres in width, which means it can only belong to a dog, a wombat or a tiger. And it's not from a wombat, because the plantar pad of the manus is not big enough, and there are only four toe pads, not five. It could be from a wild dog, but again the plantar surface points to a tiger, and – and this, thinks M, is the deciding factor – the spaces between the claw and digit are narrow, as is the space between the digit and the main pad. A dog, he knows, would leave an unmistakably large space between the digit and main pad. What is he to think? The tiger – why not? He casts around for another print, something by which he can gauge the gait of the animal and so her size. And he is in luck, for at the far end of the muddy patch, some eighty-five centimetres distant from the spoor, is another print. And looking at it M decides that – yes – as the file had said, the animal is fully grown. After a thorough inspection he confirms his earlier hypothesis: yes, she has passed this way. He stops and sits a while on his pack, passes his good eye over his surrounds. So, he thinks, what were you doing around here, my tiger? Passing through, yes, for there's nothing here to stop for, but headed where? Back down to the lake by the looks of it, but which way? Not by the route I've taken. A secret way perhaps, only for initiates. Again he feels his spine grow strong, and imagines for an instant that beneath the swelling his eye has narrowed, yellowed, deepened.

M turns back to track the tiger. She is a strange beast for she has taken care to avoid the pad, crossing it only when she has to. From what he sees, he cannot even be sure she is travelling in a definite direction. Here she shows up, and there – where he would have expected her – she disappears. He wonders if she has a map in mind. Perhaps, he thinks, the lonely years have soured in her, soured her sense of smell so that now she madly wanders through the scrub, pulled one way by one scent, one way by another.

Soon the lake and its dark rim of pines are in sight, and M finds himself walking over a boggy flat razed the night before by his rifle scope. He studies a small heap of freshly dug earth, and wonders what the animal could have been digging for. At one stage the track takes a sharp turn to the right, a seemingly senseless turn, and only when he comes across a fresh litter of wallaby scats does he understand. Then he loses the track, loses it. She has turned up onto hard ground, over rock fields, and he has lost her. M follows her up, guessing that she is eventually headed for the far side of the dolerite wall, beyond which runs a long and narrow button-grass corridor: a feeding ground. As he climbs, zigzags, over the rock field, it begins to rain. Lightly at first, but then a little harder. His boots slip on the rocks, and he moves slowly with his monovision, testing each rock with his weight before pressing on. His bad eye stings. Soon, he tells himself, I will stop and rest.

All afternoon he walks. He circumnavigates the giant wall, leaves it behind. He picks up the tiger again, or thinks he has, but with the rain fast eroding all prints he can no longer be so sure. He reaches the button-grass at dusk and quickly finds a spot to camp. At night he sits and watches. The rain clears, the clouds clear too. Under his night-vision the stars are mandalas of burning white light, and when he breathes, his cold misty breath is luminous. Finished waiting, he retires to his tent and changes out of his wet clothes, burrows into his sleeping bag. If I still had her track, he thinks, I'd never sleep. I'd follow her through the night.

He wakes to another cold morning and dresses in all his clothes. He does not like this cold, the way he needs to wear thermal gloves so that he can bear to touch the things around him. If he had a choice, he would always work in the tropics, and for a moment he wonders where his next job will take him . . . Indonesia, Hawaii, Galapagos. It is so cold he cannot imagine what it must be like to feel warm. A story told to him once, years ago, comes to mind and only now does he appreciate it: a colleague knew an old man, a sculptor living in Wales, who was so much a part of the weather around him that he would up from his warm kitchen and take his chair out into a nearby field to sit and wait for snow. You could feel snow in the air — apparently.

Once dressed and packed he drops down onto the button-grass, ready to begin anew. If he is lucky – and what is luck? – he will pick up the track again today. If not, he will set snares and the last of his traps, and wait once more for dusk.

Lunch, and he is not lucky. Afternoon, and the grass corridor dwindles away. According to his photographs, blown about in his hands so that he needs to anchor them to the ground with small stones, he has reached a cul-de-sac of sorts, and unless he wants to back-track the length of the corridor, he will have to brave a crescent of slopes so steep another man might call them small cliffs. What to do? What to do? The tiger, he thinks, would she have come this far? Or did she peel off earlier, inveigled by her phantom mate? He needs time to think. On the photograph he locates his runs. He sees that if he goes over the top he will come out néar a couple of runs he set some ten days back. Ah, his beautiful titanium traps ... ha! And in that moment his mind's eye sees quite clearly a thylacine, with its head turned away, black stripes huddled over one of his traps: caught. And for this reason, and almost this reason alone, M decides to move on, on and on.

He climbs. The blackened rocks are wet and slippery. He edges along a ledge, gripping crevices in the rock face with crooked fingers, crushing alpine ferns. Then it happens, the surprise: the world drops out from underneath him and he falls, tumbles, rackets down the slope, ricochets between tree trunks, arms flailing. Time suspends itself and as he falls he thinks, with some degree of bemusement: Is this it? Is this, right now as it's happening all around me, has it come to this?

Somewhere far off he hears a thud.

Then time clicks in, animates, and the world begins again. Pain is reborn, not a sharp pain, but a dull soupy pain that fills his head and makes him slow to think. I am lying on the ground, my cheek rests on hard wet rock. It's raining soft. See how each drop splashes off the rock. He does not think to move, to try to lift his head. He is almost happy there, immovable in the wet. He lies on the rock and lets the rain fall. A giant ant wanders by his eyeball. A little water collects beneath his nose and he breathes through one upturned nostril.

How long he lies, he does not know or care. Time has started, yes, but she, too, goes slowly. He rests his open eye. He could rest here forever. He feels his belly rise and fall with each slow breath, rise and fall. Rise and ... fall ... nothing to do with him. He is comfortable, the rock is his mother's soft and warm bosom; he can smell her. He lies and feels his belly rise and fall. He lets it rain.

The rain stops. It changes. Something else falls and rests against his cheek. After a while he opens his eye. Is it snow? Is this snow?

Is it? Could be. His eye closes. Eye open, and he thinks he sees the tiger, standing over in the shadows, studying him, and then he watches as she slouches toward him, curious, one step at a time, until she is so close he can feel her warm breath on his cheek. But her breath is sweet, and she does not guzzle at his throat, and that is when he realises he must be dreaming, or hallucinating, and that something strange is going on.

Now M hears his mother's voice, her gentle voice: 'Time to go now, time to go.' They are standing in the kitchen, a kitchen with a chessboard floor, and he is a boy wearing his blue and yellow football uniform; his mother has already collected her car keys and straw sunhat. He is eating chocolate biscuits and doesn't want to move. He doesn't feel like football today. But his mother doesn't listen to him, and starts to go outside. He wants to stay, but knows she'll be angry with him if he doesn't go to the car. He is sitting at the kitchen table with a packet of biscuits and he can hear his mother pulling out of the garage, up to the top of the driveway. She'll be angry if he doesn't go now, won't she.

M blinks. He is lying on cold hard rock and his head aches. He scans his body to feel where it hurts. Nothing is broken. What he should do is move. He hauls an arm up to feel his head. Sticky, blood. When he brings his hand to his eye he sees blood and snow. He should go now. Gingerly, he tries to get up. His pack holds him down. At first he wants to unbuckle the pack, but no, he remembers (and he does not know, but has to remember) that he should never lose the pack. He rolls onto his stomach, and with a monumental effort lifts himself onto all fours. For a few minutes he pauses, dumb, and then, chin down, he slowly moves his head from side to side. He crawls along the rock until it comes to an end, peers over. The button-grass, now piebald, is not far below him. He looks around.

This new world is sunless, or perhaps the sun has thinned out to cover the whole sky. The faint blue of dusk is in the air, which means he should hurry. Should, but can't. He tries to think: up or down, or stay where I am? Down, down where he can set up the tent and keep the snow off him. Keep warm. He crawls over the edge of rock he is on and wraps his arms around the thick branch of a gum, then swings his legs out to lock around the trunk. As he swings, pain flushes through him; he freezes, clings. Slowly, slowly, he manoeuvres himself down the trunk, and after a century he arrives on the ground. He finds he can stand, and soon after he finds he can walk.

What he does next will only ever be an oblique memory: a drunkard's dream. He will pick his way through the button-grass, turn up a gentle rise and camp beneath an overhanging slab of dolerite. There he will manage to keep his things dry. He will feed himself chocolate. He will collect sticks and shave into their dry centres with his knife. He will light a fire using his flint and some cotton wool. He will warm some water on the fire, drink a bit and let the rest cool a little before cleaning his head wound. He will strap his head with an elasticised bandage. He will keep himself warm. He will sit by his fire with his sleeping bag around him and watch the flames, intone his times-tables and stay awake. Everything beyond his little cave will disappear beneath a layer of fine white snow and sitting there, quiet now, he will declare himself a long way from home.

Burgeoning day, and M decides it is safe enough to sleep. He turns away from the white world and shields his face. When he wakes he aches all over, and realises his head has not yet cleared, the bad eye not subsided. Looking at his watch he sees that he has slept for six or so hours. Slept like a stone. He gathers himself together and crawls out of his tent, blinks in the bright light. The white world: surely he has never been this way before. Look, a white horizon wavering against a mineral grey sky. Listen.

And even in his groggy battered state M does not forget where he is and why he finds himself sitting in the snow. Below him lies the white corridor that runs off the snow-tipped dolerite wall, beyond which lies a lake. Yes, the snow has changed things, even patchy melting snow changes things. How easy it would be to lose one's bearings in the white world, to look straight at a landmark and think you'd never seen it before; not to recognise your own house or your own hand. That's how school groups got lost, and backpackers: bedazzled. And there, huddled in the sharp cold, M recalls with horrible clarity the times he had wandered off as a child, and lost himself. Sometimes he would only need to stray five metres from his mother's side and suddenly he'd be in a glaring, bustling, giant's world, where nobody cared about him, and some even frowned at him, including gnarly old women who clicked their teeth in disapproval. Around and around he'd look, then spy a woman in a blue dress and follow her for a while, down the next aisle or up the escalator, and when he'd finally catch up with his mother in the blue dress and tug at her side, she'd spin around and stare at him: now some horrible other woman with orange lipstick and a cigarette in her mouth. She'd either frown and pull herself away, or bend down and smile a horrible smile, cooing, 'What's wrong, darling? Are you lost, honey?' And he'd be incapable of speech and nod his head, at which the woman in the blue dress would sigh and take his hand and lead him over to a different woman again, a hundred-year-old lady with floss-pink hair, who would put him in a room with the other lost children and give him a lollipop to suck on. He never talked to the other lost children; the room robbed them all of speech. From out of the sides of the building he'd hear his name called, repeated three times. Eventually his real mother would open the door, looking all hot and tired, and get down on her knees, hold him by the shoulders and ask him if he was OK. She'd thank the old lady, shrugging – 'He does it all the time.'

Some said staring into the abyss was the worst thing possible, but in his little cave M thinks otherwise: at least the abyss is contained, with towering sides, but when you are lost the nightmare is truly infinite. He'd known grown men to break down crying when they'd lost their way. It was a sorry sight, to see a soldier cry. The missing man, he wonders, was it snowing when he'd lost himself? Did the white world claim him as one of its own? Was he lost in perpetuity, a condemned man, and if so, what heinous crime could have deserved such punishment? Perhaps the missing man had given up, made himself a new home? And he wonders if the children will ever send for help should he, M, fail to return. Their father might like a companion, a playmate. He can hear the girl now: 'No, don't call. Let's make him stay up there – anyway, he told me he likes it, he told me he'd like to stay, true.' She could be persuasive, that clever girl ... And the sleeping woman, what did she care? By what dreamy calculus should a stranger survive and her beloved disappear? He wouldn't be surprised if she sacrificed him: who ever said you had to throw a rope to a drowning man? He remembers a man, a lawyer, who he met in a sailors' bar in Amsterdam. This lawyer had seen a woman throw herself off a bridge, and – as he'd cleverly explained – he hadn't felt the need to stop and help.

M thinks these things and feeds himself, admires the gleaming white corridor. Perfect for prints. Imagine: a neat set of prints running all the way up the middle of the corridor, an invitation to treat. But not today, no, not today. Today he will recuperate. He hasn't the energy to walk in the snow, and besides, if he did he'd need all his wits about him: potholes, traps, hidden dangers. No, he'll spend the rest of the afternoon in his cave. After all, he reminds himself, he is patient, and he can wait.

For two long days a fine snow sifts over the white world. M stays where he is, grows strong. He shoots a wallaby and roasts it over a fire. On the third day the sun reclaims the sky, the clouds vaporise and M descends into the corridor. He navigates assiduously, and with his good eye watches every step while his other eye is swollen closed. When he comes across a puddle of snow, he pauses to inspect for prints, but otherwise he forges directly ahead, back to the escarpment. He walks and camps. One evening he notices a eucalypt chopped off at the stump and, curious about this blatant sign of human intervention, he carries out a quick reconnaissance of the area. Yes, a trapper's hut. A collapsed trapper's hut, replete with an ancient billy, seamed-glass beer bottles, and a slew of handmade nails. This is where the brave brute men of the past used to pass their winters – and look at it now, expired. Done with. He spends the night in the dark remains of the hut, cleans up the billy and gets a fire going. There are night-noises, and the fire throws night-visions. For a moment, and only a moment, a vestigial fear returns, and he recognises it as the fear of being hunted. To comfort himself he puts the rifle scope to his eye and covers the entrance to his sleeping spot. Nothing can get at him, now he is safe.

—

His theories on the intransigent girl and Sleeping Beauty cannot be tested. M is a professional, and he returns to base as agreed. But he is a beleaguered professional, a soldier dropping back from the front line, only to find himself in the blood-soaked, rat-infested trenches. His eye still bothers him, and his head wound has not healed. He has not found his prey. And so he falters. He falters when he sees, parked before the little house, a purple bus and a dirty white station wagon. He falters when he sees a tepee planted in the paddock, a tattered rainbow flag tied to its bamboo centre pole, and all around tents thrown out like spores. And he falters when the front door opens and a berry-brown man in a green velvet dress walks out and waits to meet him.

'Hi.'

M gets out of the car, nods.

'Hey, you alright, man? You OK?'

'OK. Long trip.'

'Did they get at you, man?'

Who? 'Had a fall.'

The young man in the dress looks like he doesn't believe him.

'Whatever you say, man.'

A girl with dreadlocks and a cow-hide patchwork skirt screeches from the tepee: 'Free!'

'Free,' says the dress-wearer, raising his hand like Chief Running Bull.

'Martin David,' says M.

'Om shalom.'

Yeah.

Now what? Now what. M takes his pack into the house. There are visitors. The girl, he sees, is standing on the bent knees of an older girl, a girl-woman, who might just be eighteen, with shorn hair, pierced cheek and beatific smile. Their arms are locked at the elbows and Sass is leaning back, dipping her hair down. When he comes into the fire-lit room she arches up.

'Oh, hi. Hey everybody, this is Martin David, like I told you.'

The faces around the room, there must be five of them, look and smile, a few raise their hands as if to say, 'So of all the places on the planet, here we all are.'

'What happened to your head?' asks Sass.

This is interesting: they prick up their ears.

'Had a fall. Nothing to worry about.'

'How come your eye's all funny?'

'Caught a stick in it.'

'Gross.'

'Where's your mother?'

She unfurls, says upside-down, 'Where do you think.'

Yes, the mother is asleep. He goes to the bathroom and examines his wounds, his pus-caked eye, takes a hot shower and changes his clothes. Outside he watches the reddening sunset. Free crosses the paddock and invites him to eat in the tepee. 'We've got pots and pans and can cook for twenty.' M asks if he can eat in his room. 'Sure man, sure.' As night falls the house empties, someone starts to beat a drum. He sees they are building a bonfire, dark wandering shapes bringing wood. Is that the girl he sees, holding her brother's hand? He rests by the fire inside the house and after a while the girl-woman with the shorn hair brings him a big plate of food.

'Here you are,' she says, smiling.

'Thanks. Martin David's the name.' She's a pretty girl, pretty-pretty; sleek as a cat.

'Shakti,' she says.

'So, how long are you staying?'

This is a question she doesn't like; the smile stiffens. 'Who knows. Festival's over and we're following the rainbow, you know. Yeah, we pay our respects.'

Respects?

Evidently that's all she thinks she needs to say. 'Om shalom.' She leaves.

Although he is tired he is not ready to sleep. Outside, the drum beats steadily, rising and falling. He goes to the back door and looks out to the paddock. The others are all around the fire: he can see two silhouettes dancing some kind of whirly jig. Perhaps it is because he is beleaguered, or perhaps it is because he is reckless, and whatever it is he does not care, he finds himself crossing the driveway and stepping over a discarded tin drum, onto the fringe of the paddock. Approaching the group, he prepares once more for an introduction, his specialty (I am always being introduced). This evening Martin David, Naturalist, he will be one of them.

The faces on the far side of the fire are the first to see him navigate his way through the ragwort. They look up, carry on. Free is there, back to back with the girl in the patchwork skirt. Around her neck is a sarong, and in the sarong M can make out the wispy crown of a sleeping baby. The cat-girl is there too, and Sass is snuggled tight between her thighs. And Bike? Where is the boy? There, poking a stick into the embers, deep in concentration.

M towers on the outside of the circle. The person in front of him, not having heard his stealthy approach but

105

having noticed a face opposite look up, turns and makes some room. M squats down, hold his hands out toward the flames. He smiles at Sass and the cat-girl; the cat-girl smiles back. Bike says 'Hi'. This is not a circle where names need to be given. The glowing end of a joint bobs from hand to hand, and a boy-man with a black tattoo wrapped around his wrist says, 'That joint is running round like a racing car in slow motion.' Yeah, they laugh at that. The talk goes on, there is a problem with the bus, it seems, and someone is going to have to go into town to get it fixed. Who'll go. Who's got any money. The place is full of rednecks and inbreds. Don't make the mistake of going to the pub – remember Johnny got his head kicked in. And scruff some food while you're there. Yeah, OK, we'll go then. Will ya. Yeah, get a mullet up ya. Ha. And then a girl starts chanting and a guitar emerges. Some sing, some listen. 'From big things little things grow ...' A big billy of chai goes on the fire. Quietly, a hand-entwined couple shuffles off, disappears into a tent. A joint is passed to M and, because he is on the job, he passes it on. He sees Shakti ruffle Sass's short hair, ruffle as she listens to what the fellow next to her has to say. There is mention of an action out Tarkine way, where the Road to Nowhere is being put through. Yeah, someone knows someone out there, yeah, that's right.

Bike, meanwhile, has attached himself to the tattooed boy, and is rubbing his pointed firestick along the grooves in the sole of his new friend's boot. 'Everything is about energy,' says Bike's friend, 'it's all about transformation of

energy, I mean, everything is transformed. Jarrah Armstrong
had it right: energy and matter, that's what it's all about.
No beginnings and no ends . . .'

'Bodies have an end, you fucking genius,' says another.

'Dust to dust, my fine friend, and dust is earth and
earth is beautiful, and the rest, the real thing, that goes on
too.'

'Hallelujah, brother, yeah, I'm going to live forever . . .'

'Sadly . . . sadly it's true. Even you, excuse for an entity
that you are, even you will go on.'

'Cheers.'

Ha. The immortals laugh, slowly exhale.

M does not talk. If everything is transformed then what
is extinction? He could ask but tonight he does not want
to open his mouth, tonight he wants to listen. He doesn't
even want to understand, only listen, he wants the sounds
of voices and laughter and music to pass over and around
him. For a moment he is tempted to take the hand of the
woman sitting next to him, but the moment passes. The
little girl and her brother fall asleep. Eventually he decides
to leave, and when he does, he rises and departs without
formalities. The moon is full and heavy and he needs no
torch to find his way. Back inside, lying in the narrow
bed, he can smell the wood-smoke on him, on his clothes
and in his hair, and quickly he sinks into sleep.

In the morning he finds the gentle Shakti reading on
the floor by the bookcase. He does not like to see her in
the house.

'Morning.'

She holds up the book. 'Jarrah Armstrong,' she says. 'Listen to this ... "At a time when the planet is overrun with man, is it really so unfeasible to question whose life is more —"'

'Thanks,' he says. 'Thanks.'

She shrugs and shuts up, keeps reading. He heads for the kitchen. How long, he thinks, until they move on? Please, please mother earth, please rainbow goddess, each beautiful blithesome hour is longer than eternity.

His eye clears. Once again he saddles his pack and turns off the fire-trail, past the split gum, up onto the narrow track. The world unfolds before him. When he pulls himself up over an exposed tree root, he is not retreading old ground, even though it is old ground, but is pulling himself up onto that fine cusp between the present and the future. Everything — the cool soft dawn, the dew-wet leaves, the tiny eucalypt which may or may not survive, that breath in his chest — everything is new to him.

Then he hears it: yes, the crack of a twig. He stops. Listens. What was it? A wallaby? But no, a wallaby would make more noise. A few minutes pass before he resumes his climb, and then it happens again: a scuffle behind him, a fair way down the track, sounding like the muddy slip of a boot, a stabilising grab at the ferns. Not an animal. Then who? And why? Immediately his eyes sharpen, his hearing is vivified. Listen, smell, scan. Touch. Wait. Think now, think. Could one of the visitors have followed him, has National Parks twigged to his traps, has Jack Mindy been talking around town ... is it Jack himself or one of the rednecks gone mad ... a business rival ... M countenances these possibilities in a split second, but comes to no conclusion. What to do? He makes a rough noise to suggest he is moving forward, but stays where he is. He will lie in wait. He climbs out of the deeply etched track, into the thick scrub and, scrambling low on all fours, works his way down the escarpment. There it is, the intruder again. Whoever is following him is not a professional, and with this realisation M rests a little easier. Down again, getting close. M feels his heart thumping but does not panic, remains efficient. Now he is alive.

It is the boy he sees, red-faced and sweating, clambering like a spider over roots and rocks, fingers in the dirt. Bike! An object of fascination, and quickly, annoyance: a frustration. He is wearing his red tracksuit, and a little knapsack is harnessed on his back. Buckled to the bottom of the knapsack is a sleeping bag, tightly rolled. He moves assuredly, notes M, and seemingly without fear. Exhausted, the boy pauses for breath, takes a water bottle out of his sack and drinks, presses on. Soon he stops again, winces and grips his side. In no time he is very close, not five metres away, and M decides to show himself. Like a leopard he springs out of the scrub, jumps down onto the track.

Instantly the boy freezes. He does not scream, but is wide-eyed, terrified. They stare at one another. What did he expect, this boy? What was the stupid child thinking?

'Gotcha!' says M.

Bike relaxes, relieved to be a naughty boy.

'I'm going up there,' says Bike, wildly pointing to the dappled morning sky. 'Don't worry, I won't follow you. Promise swear to God.'

'Turn around,' snaps M, tramps over to the boy and smacks him lightly on the cheek.

A mistake. Tears well in the boy's eyes, he cries and then he blubbers. He throws himself on the ground and howls. 'Can't make me, can't make me,' he tries to say, between gulps. 'Can't make me.' Then, with the hard walk behind him, Bike loses his breath and begins to hyperventilate. M watches, waits to see if the panting child will calm down. No, not this one.

'Here,' says M and softly rests his giant hands on the boy's shoulders. 'Shhh now, shhh. Big breath, big big breath ...' He slips off his pack and takes the boy in his arms – anything to calm him down. How tiny he is, and how warm. 'Shhh, it's OK ... it's OK now, all done, all done ...' And now M remembers that his own mother used to say exactly that, 'Shhh now, all done, all done ...' And many times he had buried his head in her soft fat chest and believed that, if she said so, it really was all done, and all really would be well – mountains would be moved. He holds the boy to his chest and feels the little shoulder blades rise and fall, until finally – finally! – the breath modulates, settles down.

'Let's go then,' says M, pulling away. 'Let's go.'

He'll have to take the boy back. He doesn't want to,

but it would distract him to know the boy was wandering around. Yes, he'll have to take the boy back.

In the ute Bike is silent. M doesn't ask questions, doesn't speak. What the boy dreamt was his own business. But when the house is in sight M breaks:

'So when did you get in?'

'After you went to sleep,' says Bike, staring ahead. Then he turns and grins, 'Brrrr, cold but.'

M stops by the top of the driveway and the boy climbs out.

'See ya,' says Bike.

M nods, swings the ute around. Driving past he sees Bike turn and wave him on.

Again, the escarpment. Again, he climbs. Already the sun is high in the sky, and M calculates a good half-day has been lost. But he does not resent this lost time, nor this extra work the boy has forced upon him. No, he is a professional, and so on this second ascent he will, once more, be the natural man: ready, alert and unencumbered. Once more the world will unfold before him. Once more ... These are the things he reminds himself of as he climbs, and in the reminding he recognises the effort he is making: no, despite his best intentions the world is not in fact unfolding before him, instead it is clogged all around, and with every step he is pushing his way through, only to find himself back in the sorry spot where he began. Today his pack is heavy. And to make matters worse, M finds himself cluttering his head with thoughts of the stowaway boy. Stowaways: chance-takers and desperadoes. He supposes the boy had wanted to find his father, or perhaps he had just wanted to be free of the house, to climb the beanstalk into the fabled giant's land, where magic beans grew at leisure, and where treasure could be found. What a thought – where treasure could be found.

Stop, have a cool drink.

Ah, at last the plateau, at last some open space. Pack down, he smears himself with shit and prepares to descend into the valley. But what he lacks now, he feels and knows, is conviction, and he also knows – because it has happened before – that there is no way to talk himself out of this skittish state. Reasoning, evaluation – it feeds upon itself. Other hunters, men he'd once met, used to think this mood gave off a rank human scent and to avoid its onset they would forbid all talk of matters human. For two long hot weeks – and how hot! – that party had made its way through the jungle, grunting now and then when the time came to stop for food, pointing out possible tracks, shaking heads in disagreement. When one fellow had bemoaned the hot weather and its desultory effect on his wife back home, he'd been sent from the evening circle, and no-one was allowed to look him in the eye for two days. But on this long cool afternoon even the salve of superstition has come to mind too late and M knows he will have to push through what has already begun and wait till nightfall, when at last, and only then, he will be free to call on the mother of all salvation: sweet loss of consciousness. Until that glorious time, though, he has no choice but to carry on.

He carries on.

The sun before him glowers low and gigantic on the horizon; he walks into it squinting. When he spies a possum on an exposed gum bough he takes a careful practised aim and shoots it, then skins the thing and singes the carcass with burning bracken to disguise his own hand, and suspends it over one of his beautiful traps. He eats. At night he watches over a thin hairy shank of tussock grass. Three wallabies come out to graze, and a pademelon trips by, but nowhere the tiger. Hours pass and his trap explodes: he finds he has caught himself a devil. What a noise! He shoots it for some peace and quiet. And then, finally, finally, it is time to call off the unconvinced hunt, to take some sleep. Never has he so looked forward to crawling into his sleeping bag, to rolling over onto his side and closing his eyes, to closing out the world. Sweet, sweet sleep.

A fresh day, fresh days. Feathered clouds and a light sporadic rain. He walks out past the resting spot beneath the dolerite, through the pine forest, beyond the lake. Now as he walks he once again imagines himself as the tiger: after food and shelter. He examines every muddy patch for prints, surveys the slopes for dark quiet lairs, trails his god-eye through the scrub, looking for broken twigs, flattened grass, droppings, freshly dug earth, fresh kills, a punctured skull, even clumps of hair. He travels as he imagines the tiger would travel – from one feeding ground to the next. Gone

is his nagging sense of discomfort, his lack, long gone.
Instead he is – once more, once more, ever more – the
natural man. And when his imagination fails him, when
he can't quite decide which pad to follow, which way to
go, he drops his pack and gets down on his hands and
knees and looks around. Sniffs, pulls cool air across his
nasal membranes. Is still. Then the decision is made, and
he carries on. He does this for days, patiently and without
success. The yellow nights, too, leave him bereft. But he
persists, as he knows the tiger persists: without expectation.

In the moonlight something white, something close to
phosphorescent, rests in a little pile beside a gum whose
roots droop over a rock like the tentacles of an octopus.
Bones, he decides, and goes to inspect. He finds a little
pile of bleached white porous bones. Looking at them he
knows they are human bones, but he picks one up and
examines it, just to make sure. He has found bones. He
sees they have been pulled from under a screen of fallen
branches, from their hiding place. He scrabbles through
the branches, finding other bones, but not the skull. He
takes off his pack and arranges the bones in groups according
to size. A rib. Tibia. Fibula. Scapula. A tiny metacarpal. For
no reason he taps two bones together and listens to their
sound. He digs into the ground. This was Jarrah Armstrong,
he thinks, this is a dead man. He measures a rib against
the side of his own chest. Those bones that have strayed,
pulled away by devils, he gathers together and returns to
the pile. Again, he looks for the skull. Each bone he studies
closely, looking for any tell-tale chips, the mark of a bullet.

They are fairly clean, so he guesses there must be an ant's nest nearby. A tuneful 'Are You Lonesome Tonight?' plays in his head and he thinks of the drinkers in the pub. None of the bones before him seems to have been hit, but he knows there must be other bones, and once, there were organs and flesh. Before he leaves he marks his exact position on a photograph with a small cross and in the margin he pencils in the initials J. A. Here lies J. A. May he rest in peace. Later, he thinks, I will come back and collect him. Later, when the job is done.

This devotion to the hunt is soon rewarded. A strange thing happens: one morning he is taking a piss not more than two metres from his tent when he sees – surely not – a print. Yes, it's a thylacine forefoot (Jesus Christ Mary Mother of God). The print is quite deep, the five toes – yes, all five – are clearly marked in the moist earth. The animal must have been resting on it. But, stranger still, he can't find any other prints. It's as if she had positioned herself on rocks and grass, and then stuck out one paw to leave him a message. And what message might that be? he wonders. Is it a game – has he all along been at the mercy of a merry trickster? Or is she lonely, shyly appealing to a misguided sense of fraternity? Or, a tempting thought, is his tiger curious, too curious for her own good? Has she made her first mistake?

He returns to his pack and studies his photographs, takes an inventory of his traps and snares. He slings his rifle over one shoulder and checks the safety catch. Then he sets about finding the animal's track. He examines a three-metre radius around the print in intimate detail, taking care not to befuddle the evidence with his own giant limbs. It is not as hard as he expected, and after half an hour he has a second print, and soon a third. The tiger is headed south-west, and judging by her light step she is moving at a reasonable pace. If he stays with her he might be able to catch her when and where she stops to rest. He drops down to the right of her track, downwind. He moves quickly, surely. He does not stop for lunch but eats scroggin as he goes. She is predictable now, this tiger, and he wonders if she is leading him into some trap of her own. Would a tiger kill a man? It hasn't happened before, not that he knows of, but it is possible: if she was crazed, she could lure him into some secret spot and then – from behind, or from above – launch herself at his throat, rip it out. Like taking candy from a baby.

He quickens his pace. The rain has stopped and a tallow sun filters through the grey clouds. Everything is wet; blue-grey, brown or green. He checks his watch: two and a half hours until dark. He marks his position and the time on his photograph and moves on. He has covered a lot of ground already today, has even lost the track once or twice, and found it again, but he does not feel tired, not at all. When he comes to a fallen log he crosses it easily: up one, down two, takes it in his stride (yes, she has been here – see the deep landed imprint of her forefoot, even with claws). Through the tussock grass he moves at a slow jog. In a gnarly patch of scoparia he lifts his arms to shield his upper body and slithers, brusquely, catching himself now and then, tearing himself away. To be quick, to be quick. All along he stops to take his position, so that he will always know where he is, and how best to find his way out. This awareness of his exact location, coupled with his sharp and natural eye, equips him with the hunter's greatest weapon: a sense of immediacy, a complete understanding of why space is time. I am here, he thinks, I am right here, right now. He is ready for anything.

High above, the light seeps from the sky, and the world below prepares for night: some retire – the flies, the snakes, the birds – while others rouse. M does not stop. For fifteen minutes he pauses to eat and rest a little. He washes his face. Then his night-vision is strapped on and he picks up the track again. With an overcast sky his limey-vision is poor, and after nearly tripping himself up he queries his unstoppable decision, but soon enough it is ratified and he presses on. Who is he to stop when all around the citizens of the night bustle on.

Come midnight he finds himself in sight of the pine-rimmed lake, a great glowing pool of water. She likes it here, thinks M, and he wonders why she keeps returning to this area. Has she a lair, a young one too big for her pouch but too weak to travel? Is there a mate, and not a phantom mate, but one feeble, dying in some small hidden cave? Does she kill for others as well as for herself? And now in the chill open night he allows himself a fantasy: Is

117

there an entire tribe of tigers — so crafty that they have avoided the human gaze for years, and — oh, an underground tribe of tigers — perhaps that wombat burrow over there is a tunnel leading to a complex maze, an Atlantis ... And who is his tiger but an emissary, sent by the council of elders to report back on the sorry state of affairs above ... But what do they eat, these underground beasts, have they developed a taste for worms and microbes, for the elements of decay ... Or is she an exile of this underground world, an escapee? Is her eternal wandering a form of punishment? Perhaps she has come to make amends ...

Soon this fantasy is exhausted and M stops to take a bearing. He can't be far behind her now. The pad he is on bypasses the lake, skirting along the top of the nearby ridge so that the glowing water is a distant thing, too dangerous to be close to. Where is she headed? When will she stop? And now he sees her plan: the pine forest. Into the pine forest he goes.

This is no god's country, this is god-forsaken: it is perfect and precise. Perfect thousand-year-old trees, their lowest feathered branches almost tip-tipping; an open, soft and fragrant floor; the hard petals of each pine cone divisible by the golden mean. It is cold in here and dark, too, freckled with the faintest light. No, no tracks can be left on this hallowed ground, not even by the wind. So, this is where she has chosen to bring him ... Walking slowly he feels the pine needles brush against his arms, his cheeks. He stops and quietly lowers his pack. He has traps set in here, he hasn't forgotten (how could he forget!), and he needs to ascertain exactly where they are. If I can, he thinks, I'll steer the tiger to them. He looks around: from where he is sitting there is no apparent end to the forest, no end in sight. And while he has been careful to estimate his point of entry, and the distance he has travelled – how many metres and in what direction – the perfection of the place he now finds himself in has wiped out his instinctual sense of direction, just as if a heavenly hand had passed over a compass and left its face bare. Here it is cold and dark.

He patrols the forest, methodically working his way inward, around one diminishing perimeter and then the next. There is no point doing anything else until he can pick up the track again, and that may take days: she has a choice of a thousand exits. He feels he should stay. A little later he hears something, but can't distinguish what it is, and after listening for ten still minutes he moves on. At the ready. There is no reason, he knows, to be afraid, but he cannot ignore his childhood fears of mean dark forests, of Hansel and Gretel and psychokillers. But they are only childish fears, like a fear of mice, and almost as soon as he has remembered them, the fears subside. He spies a glint of light within a tree, at eye-level, over to his right. Ah, one of his plastic strips? Now, be careful. There are traps about. And they must be empty, hungry, for all is quiet, and no decay-stink abounds.

M walks, rifle at the ready. At the ready. He walks for an hour, two hours, three ... at the ready. But he is not ready when a luminous shape cuts in front of him – he sees it cross the pine alley he is in, some twelve metres ahead. No more than a yellow shadow. As big as a tiger. Which way? It was moving east. He moves east, three wavering alleys across, which he calculates as being fourteen metres and so makes a mental note. Looking, scanning. There it is again, further away now, weaving through the pines and flashing like a semaphore. M takes a path parallel to the animal, feels his heart thump. He works his way closer. To get a shot he'll need a clear short line of fire. Good, good, go that way ... towards the traps, very good. M follows. At the ready, at the ready. Closer now, he can almost make out the animal: Are they stripes on those disappearing lower haunches, or is it a trick of the light? But what else could it be? Whatever it is, he plans to disable it. Now is no time for thinking.

And then the moment, for which he could never have been ready, is upon him. On their line of travel he has eclipsed her, so that any second now she will pad from one pine to the next, right before him, and in that split-second, in that tiny space between the trees, he will at last have his shot. He drops down on one knee and lifts the rifle to his shoulder; holds still. He breathes and does not think. He sees everything. Now, any second now, things are almost in their place.

Now!

The rifle explodes against his shoulder: once, twice, reverberates. And straight away he realises he has missed, that for no good reason the tiger has changed her path at the very last instant, side-stepping his bullet into the phalanx of pines. He charges forward and lets off a round of shots in quick succession, but this belated hopeful measure proves to be no good. The luminous creature has taken flight and disappeared.

Later he calls to mind the moment he saw her: he is sure she never saw him.

He scours the east rim of the forest for the next two days, trying to pick up her track. A heavy rain falls on the late afternoon of the second day, heavy and full, and with it M's hopes of finding a print are washed away. It is when this deluge starts that he gets down on his knees, one man on the plateau, and – speechless – holds his head between his hands.

He is homeward bound and empty-handed. He never wants to travel the plateau again and he wonders if this is what it means to fail, to be a failure. He never wants to spend another day walking with the rain blowing in his face; he never wants to eat cold food; he never wants to sling on a pack or peg down a tent. He resents tightening his boots. To fail? This time it seems he will fail. He repeats this: I will fail. He says it out loud: I will fail. Then again, louder: I will fail. I will fail. The will to failure. Ha, at last he has found it, the world seen from within, it is the will to failure and nothing else. Suddenly everything makes sense.

He thinks: I will cosset myself in failure.

He thinks: My patience has worn thin.

He thinks: The game is up.

Now he has reached the top of the steep track leading down the escarpment and he pauses a fraction before plunging forward. His arms writhe, his boots skid. And on! Away! Leave it all behind. In the ute he is restless, and when a roaring rattling log truck refuses to let him overtake, speeding up every time he edges out of the lane, he recklessly puts his foot down and, blaring his horn, blindly hurtles past. Eventually he makes it to the house, and he sees that the tepee is gone, the marauders have moved on. The boy opens the door and lets him in. M takes a long steamy shower until the water starts to run cold. He scrubs himself with soap. The water soothes him, wears him down.

Where is the woman?

'Gone to town.'

'And your sister?'

'Gone with her to the doctor's.'

The boy is glum. Any fun at the prospect of being left alone has long since disappeared. In a fit of generosity M offers to take Bike for a drive. He sits the boy on his lap and lets him steer. They don't go far, a few hundred metres or so, and then it is time to turn around, head home. Sass and Lucy are in the kitchen. Sass is sitting at the small wooden table, swinging her ankles and peeling potatoes. She doesn't look well, and she momentarily stops peeling, coughs. Her wrists are thin and breakable. Her mother is chopping carrots on the bench-top; beside her is a large steaming saucepan. They have been quiet, the men, they have snuck into the kitchen with the intention of surprise. Bike lifts one foot and holds it in the air for five seconds, soundlessly places it down, and then the next step, followed by another pause. He is a study in concentration.

'Rarr!' Bike charges in and grabs his mother by the waist. She squeals, her hands fly up.

'You two!' she says. 'Well, that's a surprise.' She scrunches Bike's hair.

'I drove the car, I drove the car,' chants Bike.

'Liar.' Sass is sullen.

'I drove the car, I drove the car.'

'Mum!'

Lucy looks at M, then at Bike. 'Did you, darling?'

'Didn't I?' says Bike, looking to M for support.

'We went for a quick spin, just down the driveway.'

Lucy looks – happy. Sad and happy at the same time.

'Big deal,' says Sass, peels.

They eat well that night. The children finish early and, on their mother's instruction, go to their room. Again she confides she has stopped taking her pills. When he does not respond, only nods his head, she tells him that this time – this time she means it.

'Nobody knows,' she says, more to herself than to him, 'what I'm going through.'

But her spirits quickly rally and she offers him a glass of wine: Red or white? Red, he says. Red will be fine. They drink one bottle and open another. The fire keeps the room warm, comfortable. There is a silence between

123

them, but he is not concerned. He drinks and tries to forget his tiger. He lets her get far away, he lets the plateau expand a thousandfold and gives her ten-league boots. He gives her wings. Lucy, too, is quiet, her eyes on the fire.

Bike comes in, red-faced after crying. He squirrels onto his mother's lap.

'What's wrong?' she asks.

'Sass is scaring me.'

'Don't be silly, sweet. She's just playing.'

'No, no.' Bike grows agitated and shakes his head.

'Come on, now, you're a big boy. Eight-and-a-half year olds don't get scared.'

He refuses to listen, squeezes his eyes shut.

She cannot make him budge. He falls asleep, there by the fire. As soon as she tries to lift him he wakes, clings, and will not let go. He wants to sleep in her room, he wants to sleep with her. She sighs, alright then. It's late, she says, time for bed. She rolls her eyes. Goodnight. Goodnight, says M.

M sits alone by the fire. With the wine in his belly he is warm and comfortable, and the day's misgivings seem far behind him. Who is he, really, to return empty-handed? Life is hard, he thinks, but it is not in my nature to give up. That's right, he does not give up. If he'd wanted to give up he should have done so years ago. That's right, that's right, and besides, things could be worse. Yes, they could be worse. He might never have seen the tiger. He might doubt that she exists. But she exists, he has crossed

124

her path. He knows where she is. Ah, he can feel his hopes rekindling; they are wine-fuelled, he knows, but he enjoys them nonetheless. If she has wings, he thinks, then so do I. Wings! He looks at the poster on the wall, at the unicorn in the clouds, and imagines hunting in the sky: swooping down on wind currents, hiding behind storm clouds, reading the calligraphy of birds. He knows he is drunk because the dimensions of the room are unstable. It takes a great deal of effort to get into bed.

———

Bike races to answer the telephone.

'Hello? . . .

'Did you know there are two thousand million and thirty-six stars in the universe?'

Bike turns triumphantly to Sass, like he's finally settled an old score.

'And,' he insists, pushing his luck, 'there are only three animals in the whole world in every country. Your turn – guess which ones.'

M almost feels sorry for the indefatigable Mrs Mindy: let her guess.

'Wrong! Wrong!' Bike is excited. 'Go on, guess again, one more guess – last one . . .

'Wrong! Cockroaches, pigeons and –'

He's forgotten, he looks to his sister for help.

'Ants.'

'– and ants,' he says. 'OK. Hang on a minute. Bye.'

He turns to M and holds out the phone. 'It's for you.'

For him? Him?

Wary, he picks up the receiver. 'Martin David.'

And then, 'Yes, I see.'

There it is, a call from the middleman, as deceptively sudden, and irrefutable, as any call from God. A new job must be done – 'imperative, you understand'. As it happens – 'As it happens, I'll be in Sydney tomorrow. We'll meet at five.' So, well, it is decided then, they will meet tomorrow in Sydney at five.

'Who was it?' asks Sass.

'Nobody,' says M. 'Just work.'

He goes to his room and shuts the door and packs away his things. Lucy is waiting for him when he emerges.

'What's up?' she asks. He sees she is anxious.

'An emergency. They need me back in Sydney.'

'I hope everything's OK.' She has imagined the worst.

'Not too bad. Nothing terrible. They just need me for a few days to sort out a mess in the Department. Stupid, really.'

The children have crept into the hallway and are listening closely.

'So you'll be back soon then,' says Lucy.

'I'll be back.'

'I'll be back,' mimics Bike in a thick German accent. Sass punches him on the arm.

'When do you think you'll be back?' asks Lucy.

'Hopefully in a week. At the most, two weeks.' Can she tell that he doesn't know, that he is lying?

126

'He won't be gone long, kids,' says Lucy. 'Will you?'

'Don't worry about it.'

'Can I have the toothbrush?' asks Bike.

M is confused.

'From the airline,' explains Lucy. 'Not for this trip,' she says to Bike. 'They don't give them out for this trip. Only on overseas flights.'

Bike is disappointed. He has another idea: 'Can I come to the airport?'

Lucy waits. M is quick to answer. 'Perhaps another time.'

'He'll be back soon, sweet,' repeats Lucy. Like a silver medallist, she musters up a smile.

Later, when he is alone, Lucy quietly disturbs him.

'I'm sorry,' she says, crushing her shoulder against the door jamb, 'I just wanted to know . . .'

He sees she is having difficulty picking the right words.

'. . . well, about the money . . .'

Ah, the money, the pay-off. She wants to know if the payments that have been made every week since his golden arrival will now be coming to an end. The woman is a lot more practical, he thinks, than I ever gave her credit for. A mistake.

'They'll be fine,' he promises. 'I'll look into it.'

Sass asks for her photo back.

Martin David says goodbye. Lucy promises she will miss him. A feeling of warmth, actual bodily warmth, flushes through his chest and he realises that he, too, will miss her, will miss them, and this feeling doesn't leave him as he drives away, followed by Bike, who runs hard all the way to the end of the driveway.

II

There go the haphazard roadside topiaries. He drives with his window half open and lets a light mist of rain fall on his arm, inhales the sunset. When he comes to the petrol station he pulls over and goes inside. The same woman who last served him is sitting before her miniature TV, and he notices she has dyed her hair a bright shade of coppery red. He buys chocolate, thinking: When I show up this will surprise them.

Back on the road he has a second thought: he hopes Lucy likes chocolate. But who doesn't like chocolate? All women like chocolate – don't they? What he feels, he realises, is nervous. This worry about chocolate can only be the result of nerves, like a child waking up at dawn on Christmas morning, like a boy going on a first date ... It is not an uncomfortable feeling, so he allows it to continue. Perhaps he should have called ahead; after almost eight weeks' absence, perhaps he should have let them know he was coming ... This idea of a surprise, which until now had seemed a good idea, an idea designed to show him in the best light, suddenly looms in his mind as a terrible mistake, as the worst thing he could ever possibly have chosen to do. Stop, though, he tells himself, don't exaggerate. Surprises are fun. There's no harm to it. They'll be happy to see me. That's what he wants, he wants them to be happy to see him, as happy as he will be to see them. This is what makes him nervous, this loaded sense of anticipation. And what will she say? And what will he reply? One day ... one day he might lie with her in bed and confide that on the day he had returned he'd been so – nervous (Nervous! she'd laugh. You, nervous?) – that he'd contemplated turning back. He might tell her that he wondered if she liked chocolate, that he thought about throwing it out the window rather than watch her face drop at the sight of an unwanted gift. Yes, he will stroke her back when the children knock on the door and then come in with breakfast-in-bed, soggy French toast and lukewarm coffee, and he will whisper in her ear that once he worried she wouldn't like chocolate. Then he'll listen to her laugh.

That sensation of warmth spreads in his chest.

It is the driving on empty roads that does this to him, sends him into fantasy lands. Other people do it jogging or swimming or sitting on public transport; he does it driving. But he is well aware of this trickster habit, and is always careful to keep it in check: the woman, he knows, might not need him, or want him, and – most importantly – he might not want or need her. But the thought is there, he has thought that maybe one day he might like to grow old on a farm, with loved ones around (loved ones!). Absence, he has discovered, does make the heart grow fonder. (Once it has a grip on you, absence, it cannot be defeated – how can you fight against nothing, where do you aim your blows, and where can you grip if you need to claw your way out?) Anyway, one day there has to be an end to the hotel rooms, the laminated bench-tops, the checking in and out, the looking for good restaurants, the introductions, the fake women with their fake names, the telephone calls. Yes, he is glad he requested a return trip to the island, it's got to be worth a try. Yes, it's a good thing. A good thing.

Ah! At last, the driveway, at last the house. No lights are on. He toots his horn, *tooot toooot*. And once more – *toooot*. Where are they? Asleep? He knocks on the front door – *bang, bang, bang*. Waits, hears nothing. He cups his eye against the window and tries to look in, but the rainbow curtains are drawn closed and the tiny sliver of open space between them is dark and reveals nothing, only darkness. Strange. He walks around the back and notices the children's bikes, both of them, propped up against the side of the house. So then, they must be home. It occurs to him that they might have all gone out for the evening, into town perhaps (unlikely – but why not, why not?). He calls out – 'Hello! Hello! It's me! Hello!' For a second he is unsure what to do, then he decides to let himself in: he is not a stranger; when they see him they'll understand. He tries the back door but finds it locked. The window, however, is unlocked, and he jemmies it open and clambers in, landing in darkness, sprawled on the floor. Up quickly, switch on the light. And then he sees it, he stands amongst it. An animal must have been at the lounge, ripped out its stuffing and strewn it across the carpet. For some reason all the chairs have gone. On the table are bowls of mouldy withered food, and all about are black pellets, big enough to have come from rats, not mice. A largish patch of carpet before the fireplace has been burnt, the blackened floorboards show through. He sighs, and the sigh comes from a place inside him so deep nothing could be deeper. The kitchen, he sees, has also been abandoned. He tries Lucy's bedroom, first knocking on her door. He is sickened to discover there is no bed. The children's room, too, is half empty; a heap of clothes fills a corner. The walls, he sees, are still painted — scribbled and swirled. He doesn't like it. 'Hello! Helloo!' he tries again but his calls go hollow and unanswered. Outside he calls and yells, then he crosses into the paddock and calls and yells some more. Passing back through the house he switches off all the lights and locks the doors. What can he do but get in his car and leave?

Drive. It is unbelievable.

He arrives at Ye Old Tudor Hotel just as the publican is calling for last drinks. It's a Friday night and the pub is crowded, noisy, smoking. He stands at the bar and waits until the last of the beers has been pulled and pushed. Naturally, no-one speaks to him. He is not disturbed by this, because now he is living in a world where anything is possible and in order to survive he must be accommodating. Things are happening all around him, other people are carrying on doing what they have to do, but he doesn't assess them, he doesn't compare himself with his circumstances; it is a new world with which he cannot engage, its rules are not his rules, they are incomprehensible, and so – whatever happens – he has nothing to call on by which he can say he has been wronged.

'Yeah?' It's the publican.

'Have you a room, just for one night, just one night,' says M.

'One night?'

'One night.'

The publican looks at him for a long time, then reaches into a drawer below the bar and pulls out a key on a fluoro green plastic key-tag.

'You alright, son?' he says, voice low, handing over the key.

M knows then that he is not alright, not alright at all, but what he says is, 'Yeah, good thanks, mate, fine.'

He is turning away when, involuntarily, he says, 'I've just been down to the Armstrong place ...'

It is a statement, not a question, and the publican gives an 'Oh really?' lift of the brows. When he sees M isn't moving, he says, 'Cleared out.' Then, when M remains standing, he reiterates: 'Pissed off.

'Ask Mindy about it,' he adds, absolving himself.

M has had his chest scooped out. His skin has been peeled from his body. He can dislocate his jaw and fill the universe with a stone-grey roar.

The next morning he goes to visit Jack Mindy, but Jack is not at home. His wife is, though, and M turns to her

135

for answers. He sits, dumbfounded, on a dust-pink settee and listens to her talk.

'It was the girl,' she says, 'it was the girl, you see, sleeping by the fire one night – you know how cold it gets – and somehow the fire got out, a spark got into her clothes or something and whatever she was wearing, a green thing I think it was, one of her crazy get-ups, well the thing went quick-smart up in flames, just like that . . . She couldn't get her clothes off, not by herself, and the boy, bless him, he was with her, sleeping right by her – it's a miracle really – he did his best, of course, but he's only a boy and the thing was, by the time she'd rolled around screaming, with a few cups of water thrown over her, well it was pretty much too late by then and she was badly, badly burnt . . .

'And Lucy! That Lucy didn't even hear it – those pills of hers, you know her, terrible things. Thank God the boy had the presence of mind to call me, where he found the number I don't know, but he called me and told me his sister was dead and could I please come over and have a look . . . Oh God! Sorry, don't worry, she's not dead – not dead, badly burnt – laid up in the hospital and can't even move. Me, I didn't know what to do, I called an ambulance and then Jack and me went round ourselves, quick as we could. When Lucy saw what had happened she couldn't believe it, water started streaming down her face like she was crying, but she wasn't really crying, she was just standing there, with these tears running down her face. And we all went to the hospital, the boy too, and when finally the nurses told us she'd be OK and we could go home, well what did the boy do but refuse to leave – he wasn't tired that boy, full of beans – and he kicked and screamed like there was no tomorrow, until all the nurses could do was set up a cot beside the bed, so that's what they did . . .

'The next morning, Lucy and me went back to the hospital and they told us the news wasn't good, the kid had to go to the mainland to some special burns unit, they said they needed to run some tests and they wouldn't tell us any more, no matter how much we asked them . . . So then, well, Lucy got packed up and off they went, headed to the Kids' Hospital in Sydney . . . I kept in touch, mainly with the nurses, because what happened was, well, it was Lucy, you see, she finally gave up, I don't think she could bear it, losing another one . . . last straw it was . . . so she gave up . . . she couldn't function, they had to put her in a hospital too, some institution with a nice view of the harbour, you know the kind of place I mean . . . God knows where the money came from . . .

' . . . The boy? Poor chook, what could we do? Jack and me couldn't take him in, look at me, I'm too old for all that, not again . . . But, well, they put him in foster care, I mean, he's in a home and they're looking for a good family for him, a good place to go . . . There's no denying it, a black cloud's come over that family, that's all I can say, a black, black cloud . . . God bless, touch wood and God bless . . .'

He makes a quick exit. Nothing.

What he does next he does largely without thinking: he does what he has to do. He returns to town and goes to Sid's Supermarket, purchases supplies. He is standing by the check-out when two boys in khaki uniform walk in, and he recognises them from his night sitting by the fire – the two immortals.

'Hey.' He, too, has been recognised, and nods hello.

'Hey you,' says one of the boys as he pokes the girl behind the check-out in the ribs.

'Ouch!' She laughs, blushes, is suddenly fascinated by her register.

'Come on,' cajoles the boy, 'time for a smoko?'

Now she is furtive. Apart from M the store is empty.

'OK,' she says, 'just a minute.'

She runs up his bill.

Looking closely he sees the boys are wearing National Parks uniforms. He must be staring because one of them puts his hand to the embroidered emblem on his sleeve and says, 'Yeah, man, working for the government.' He leans close and whispers in M's ear: 'Searching for tigers!' Ha, the boy laughs, finds this highly amusing. M pays his bill and leaves. He goes into the hotel to deposit his key and the publican pockets it wordlessly.

'Hey cunt!' calls a drinker, the same red-faced drinker who had insulted him before. This time the drunk gets up and walks over to the bar, rests his elbow close. M can smell the alcohol on his breath.

'See you're back then, eh? Can't keep away? Yeah, don't tell me, they've got you up there looking for the bloody

Tassie tiger, eh? Where's your nancy uniform, eh? No secret, mate, everyone in town fucken knows about it.'

Ha ha ha ha.

Finished laughing, he sighs, 'Fucken cunts ... fucken waste of taxes.'

The publican keeps an eye on this.

'Another beer, mate,' says the drinker, perking up. He turns to M. 'Jesus Christ, you're a miserable son of a bitch, you'd think –'

With his right hand M reaches around to the back of the drinker's head and thumps it down hard against the bar. The man slumps, slides, unconscious.

'Piss off,' says the publican, steely voiced.

He goes.

He drives, and the car takes him back to the bluestone house. The escarpment beckons. Soon, he thinks, soon he'll be there. He wishes he was there now, up where it was calm and pure, with space enough for a man to think. Up there change was graceful: the moon waxed and waned, gums shed their leaves, the miry tarns rose – or fell. Perhaps a bough might break off in a storm, or a creek overflow after sustained and heavy rain, but even those changes, still easily accommodated, were rare. And as for the cataclysmic changes – the meteors, volcanoes and earthquakes – when did they happen? Every odd millionth year ... Not like a man's life, thinks M, if a man's life were an island it would be uninhabitable.

He will sort it all out when he gets there. Not now, now he needs to sleep.

Someone has just turned a light on in the house. Yes, he can see it! There's a light! And another! What – are they home? Could they be back home? He has lost the ability to predict, and anything is possible.

He stands outside the front door and quietly calls, 'Hello?'

He hears footsteps in the hallway – yes, watch, the door is opening.

It's Free. It's Free.

Free is wearing one of Lucy's dresses; it's hanging out below a bulky woollen jumper.

'Hey man,' says Free, 'come on in.'

Inside, Free's partner is crouched before the fireplace, balancing wood. The baby is crawling by her feet.

'Hi,' she says, quickly looking up. 'We heard the place was empty.'

'Sad story,' says Free. 'I'm taking a job up on the plateau,' he adds, 'get some money together.'

'And I'm looking after the fucking kid.'

'Some of the others have been going up too,' he continues. 'Somebody reckons they saw a tiger. National Parks wants to tag it.'

'Seen a ghost more like it,' says the girl.

'Who's complaining?' he replies.

'We're sleeping in here,' she says, 'by the fire. Sleep where you like.'

M collects an armful of clothing from the children's room

140

and takes it to Lucy's bedroom, where he roughly fashions a bed-mat. He unrolls his sleeping bag. In the bathroom he finds a plastic vial full of Rohypnol tablets and, bending over, he fills his mouth from the tap, then swallows two.

There is a plaster rosette, complicated and white, in the middle of the ceiling, and he watches it, heart slowing, the lumpy clothes beneath him, until – turning onto his side and lifting his knees to his chest – he sinks into a gentle and innocent sleep.

Up.

He needs to concentrate on every step, making a decision every time he lifts his muddy boot as to where he will put it down again: the dry rock; the far side of the tree root; midway up the wall of a deep rut. He now pays attention to such minutiae, once the province of instinct, so that other, less pleasant, thoughts do not cross his mind. But it is no good, he cannot help himself, and he is not yet to the top of the escarpment before the lamentations begin. I have been forsaken, he thinks, the world conspires against me. I try, I try, and look what happens. I did not ask for much, did I, no, other men have asked for more, and still I am denied. He listens to himself: it is disgusting, to feel so sorry for oneself. The whole thing is disgusting; he doesn't want to know about it. Worse things, he thinks, worse things can happen. But can they? Can they really? Even the solace he offers himself is barren.

By the time he reaches the plateau a pale moon is impressed high against the pale afternoon sky. He drops his pack and rests. As if under ghostly instruction he seeks out a pile of wallaby scats and makes a paste to disguise his scent. It is strange, but once this is done he senses a small measure of comfort. He stretches his arms out wide and feels the wind against his palms, then rotates his arms as subtly as a gliding bird turns its wings. The world is behind me now, he thinks, imagines himself airborne: I have left it all behind. He looks across to the ridge of gums and thinks of the soft green tiers of leaves as cloud banks. Like a plane, he flies in that untouchable realm above the clouds. But then the wind picks up and his fantasy dissolves.

For the rest of the day he vacillates between lament and the consequent desire to leave the sorry world behind. He wonders if this is what is meant by purgatory – at least, he hopes it is purgatory and not something worse. Anything, he reminds himself, anything is possible. At night, lying on the hard ground, he is plagued by thoughts of the girl, Sass, now condemned to lying down, and of her mother, who knows no better. It gets so bad that he has to stand up, walk around.

These are not easy days. To give himself some purpose, and not because he really has a purpose, he sets out to examine his traps and snares. What else can he do? There is no better option. And every time he approaches one of his creations he prepares himself for the possibility that he might find the tiger, or what is left of the tiger after the devils have done with it – stripped it of meat and bone, leaving behind only the trapped leg, or perhaps a scrap of skin. Who cares? There's a thought: he will travel with a thylacine foot as a talisman, his bastard rabbit's foot, a reminder not of the way things might be, but of the way they really are.

All of his traps are empty of tigers. He has caught air, clouds, damp, two wallabies, a currawong, a brush-tailed possum, a pademelon. The snares he comes across are also tiger-bare. Along the way he makes himself scarce, wary that the National Parks boys are also out hunting. When he can, he keeps to high and rocky ground. Breaking camp he removes every last sign of his incursion. In these uneasy days he does not check every muddy patch for signs of a print, nor does he venture off the pad to explore a possible lair. He sets no new snares and, resting by a grass run at dusk, he lays his rifle by his side. Chiefly, what he does is walk: he heaves himself along, from A to B then C; walks and sleeps. He figures that in time – given time – in time, yes, things will be different. That is as much as he is prepared to believe.

His food runs out, until all he has left is half a bag of scroggin and a handful of mung-bean seeds. Although he is far from the track that leads down the escarpment he does not worry; a man, he knows, can survive for thirty days on water alone. He spends a long becalmed night beneath a full moon which turns the world around him an eerie steel-blue, enhancing his surrounds as if they were pixels on a computer screen. Come morning M decides that he is not ready to leave, that he does not want to return. Where, for a start, would he go? No – better, he thinks, to stay where he is, where he can at least be safe and alone.

Hunger creeps up on him, crawls into his stomach and makes itself known. Although he is reluctant to pay any attention to himself he determines that eventually he will have to shoot and cook a wallaby, either that or suffer as his hunger grows. There is a small chance one of the National Parks party will discover him, yes, perhaps hear the shot or see his fire smoke, but it is a chance he will have to take. And if it must be taken, he thinks, why not take it now?

Grey dusk. A fat wallaby wanders into sight and M levels his rifle and in one shot brings it to the ground. On inspection he finds a full-grown male, with no evident defects. He skins and guts the carcass on the spot, removing the sex glands so that they don't spoil the meat. Yes, the meat itself is passable: clean-smelling (smells like meat); no muscle, bone or joint deformities; no bleeding or bruising; firm. He inspects the rib-cage, looking for nodules. Burying his hands deep in the chest cavity he finds a set of glands, and one is larger and grittier than the other. It is not a good sign, he knows, a swollen gland, and he pauses to consider whether, after all that work, after that tell-tale shot, he should throw the thing away and start again. One gland, he tells himself, hungry and cunning, what's one gland – nothing's perfect.

He carries the skinful of carcass into a hidden spot in the scrub and lays it out on a slab of rock; the rest he leaves for the devils. In a short time he has found some kindling, dry twigs and stiff dead grass, as well as a few longer, thicker sticks. He carves into these larger pieces with his knife, deep into their dry centres, so that each one looks like a feathered totem pole. He is grateful it hasn't rained that day. When this job is done he takes a small pad of cotton wool from his pack, then strikes his knife down against the tinder block that hangs from his belt – one strike, hard – and watches as the sparks catch and the cotton wool starts to smoulder. Gently, he lifts the precious pad into his kindling pyramid, an acolyte making an offering. There is no wind, and again he is grateful: he will have his fire, and the smoke spire will not carry on a breeze. He skewers small chunks of the meat onto a green stick and secures them with string. While the meat roasts he stays by the fire and is soothed by its heat. He grows sleepy; how long, he wonders, since I last ate? Since I last slept? When no answers are forthcoming he shrugs the questions away.

Eventually the meat is cooked; some is charred, some stringy bloody pink. He savours a few mouthfuls and wraps the rest in a plastic bag, sticks it in the top of his pack. He doesn't want to, he almost can't be bothered, but what he should do is break camp and move away from the smoke. Hide somewhere safe. The rest of the meat he can't eat, not until he has let it sit in his gut for a good four hours, and only then, if his stomach has not revolted, can the meat be deemed safe for consumption. So, off he goes. He walks, side-steps potholes, memorises the past: the cluster of four gums, the boulder with a black lichen birthmark the shape of England. It is an easy walk, along a flat marshy stretch running between two low ridges, and he has put a fair distance behind him when he feels – unmistakably – his stomach flush and tighten. Take off the pack. Yes, it happens again, but this time with less intensity, and he wonders if it is not food poisoning but simply a hunger pang. Is it hunger? It could be hunger. If it is hunger, then he should eat. He decides to eat. The meat, lukewarm, tastes good; salty. He wants more and so he eats more. He eats his fill.

He rinses his hands in some night-cold water and then looks for a suitable place to sleep. A springy patch of ferns tempts him, but he remembers that he is not alone and that the next day flattened ferns would give him away. Try harder. He finds an overhanging rock ledge and uses his pack, which stinks of meat, a beacon to devils and other night citizens, as a resting post. Lying against it he reaches down and takes off his boots, frees his calloused feet. How incredibly light they are, he thinks, waving his ankles from side to side, so thin and pale and light. Before snaking into his sleeping bag he has the presence of mind to mark his position on the appropriate aerial photograph. There is no need to fashion some sticks into an arrow pointing out his direction, for come tomorrow, who knows where he will go.

Nearby, a devil snorts and grunts. But M is unperturbed. He moves closer and closer towards the precipice of sleep, moving with the same determination seen in the faces of sleep's emissaries, the night-walkers, and he lets the night-noises guide him there.

He keeps himself hungry, roasting wallaby from his traps only when he has to. (What would thylacine taste like? he thinks one night as he chews on a tough piece of wallaby. Dog? It is a crazy thought, he knows, and it passes quickly.) He decides that hunger is the only thing to keep him sharp. Stiff hair grows out of his face, and he enjoys rubbing his hand over the stubble, feeling its resistance and making it move. And he finds, weeks later, that he has developed another habit: he no longer follows the rhythm of night and day, but sleeps when the urge takes him, catching a few hours at a time, here and there, be they light or dark. Like Napoleon, he thinks, who only ever slept four hours at a time ... Ha, yes, like Napoleon ... He fills the button-grass plain with steaming horses and splashing mud and all the bloody mayhem of a war ...

In those weeks of doing little more than finding food and shelter, of breathing and pumping blood and watching the clouds form and fade, the melancholia deep inside him – the bucolia – works its way to the surface like a bullet or splinter being slowly expelled from a wound. He comes to think of his fondness for Lucy and the children as an aberration, a monumental lapse in judgement, and his vision of growing old and happy in a bluestone house seems to him near laughable: he is not, he tells himself, nor has he ever been, a sentimental man. It is not in his nature. And besides, it does not matter what he had hoped for, hoping itself was an exercise in delusion, and all the hope in the world could not determine which way a bird would fly, or a leaf would fall. Things were as they were,

147

that was all. Yes, he can be quite sure of it. But in time, over days and nights, nights and days, waking and sleeping, even this adamant strength of feeling is diluted, falls away.

Slowly, slowly, he comes into his own. What he is left with is a remarkable clarity, as if all along the sun had only shone at half strength or, worse, had not even risen. Or perhaps he'd been the blind one, with a thousand fish scales layered over each eye. What he sees now is that he has been tested, steeled, and seduced, and that his true purpose is the one which he first set out to achieve: to be a hunter, to harvest the tiger. What else could it be? We all know what we are meant to do, he thinks, it is always simple. The fools among us let other things get in the way.

And so, off he goes – once more ranging forward with the trusty weight of a rifle in hand. He knows where he is headed; he will take some traps out past the pine forest, bearing north-east. Dusk, and he watches over the animal traffic; the slow tide of dawn, and he does the same. To reacquaint himself with the tiger he gets down on his knees and crawls along an open pad with his jaw dropped wide until his rough palms begin to smart and then it is best to stand back up. All this takes place with great ease, and because it is so easy he knows that it is right.

What! His freshly shucked eyes surprise him: hanging mid-air is the severed head of a possum, a demented Cheshire cat. Black flies buzz all over it; red, white and purple tendrils dangle from beneath a ruff of grey-brown fur: this handiwork is not his doing. He sees two wooden stakes driven into either side of the pad, each a metre long, and attached to these stakes, not far from the ground, are rude clumps of vine. Beneath the vine? He can't quite make it out. Look around. Up ahead lies a black wooden box, the size of a fruit box, which is capped with an overhanging and inclined black PVC shield. The open face of the box is pointed toward the suspended possum head. A black cable, partially visible through a loose cover of dirt and dead leaves, snakes between the black box and one of the wooden stakes. M steps off the pad and gathers a handful of small rocks. He tosses these rocks at the possum head – *Flash! Click-clicck whirrrr.* An infra-red photographic unit, he thinks, wild-eyed portraits and no negotiation. This time they'll see a ghost.

By the sorry look of the possum he estimates the bait was set two or three days ago, maybe four – maybe more. He avoids the infra-red trip-beam and inspects the box. Inside nestles a camera equipped with a motor-drive attachment and a bulk film magazine, a flash gun and two twelve-volt batteries connected in parallel. It is a set-up he is familiar with, an archaic one by his standards, and he guesses the National Parks crew are involved. Yes, on the underside of the box is a small plastic plaque identifying it as the property of National Parks, serial number 303A. These batteries, he knows, need to be recharged every twelve days, and he calculates that, for a few days at least, he need not expect immediate company.

He looks for signs of his new rivals and finds plenty: a tiny trampled gum, a moss scrape on a fallen log, a bent green bough at shoulder height. These men are walking carelessly, with no concern for detection. Checking his photographs he sees that he is close to a pretty spot he has passed before, a clear round tarn like a large pond or a well, fringed with flat rock and gums for shade. It had, on the occasion of his passing, made a memorable camping spot. If I were a betting man, he thinks, I'd wager I'd find who I'm looking for there. To pass the time while tracking his new prey he lays some odds, weighing up every possible variable, until he settles on twelve to one. Less likely, he thinks, that I'll learn anything new about my tiger, but who knows, and every angle must be checked.

And yes, as he peers beyond a boulder, down in the hollow he can make out two figures in khaki moving around a fluoro orange tent. From where M stands the tent looks like a lump of mutant fungus. One man, slightly taller than the other – call him Tall – goes behind a tree to take a piss, little knowing that his attempt at discretion brings him into full view of an audience. M watches him stand for an unusual length of time with his dick in his hand before finally shaking himself off, tucking it away. Twilight falls and the two men light a fuel stove: a burning point of light like a tiny earthbound star. The water shimmers. Under the cover of night M skulks closer to the camp, taking care to keep quiet and downwind. Downwind! There is no mistaking the sweet fusty smell of marijuana, only a man with no nose could miss it.

Hunched by the fuel stove, propped up against their packs, beanies hooded over their eyes, are the boys from the store. Yes, he can see clearly now – the immortals. Small is

150

fixing some instant pasta over the fuel stove. M edges closer, hides himself stock-still. He listens a long while but the boys hardly speak, and when they do their words are swallowed, low, hard to hear. At one point after their meal Tall breaks out laughing, can't stop laughing, and Small is infected and laughs along too. They're having the time of their lives, thinks M, being paid to sit up here and laugh. He sees they've strung up a hammock between two trees, and high up in another tree is tied a bulky plastic bag of rubbish. That's good. He guesses they haven't been searching for the tiger at all, and instead have been lounging around the campsite, doing the absolute minimum they can get away with, which would be to check on the photographic unit and little else. He waits and watches until Tall abruptly pulls himself up and, switching on a torchlight, goes over to open the tent. Small joins him. The point of light flies around the orange tent, then suddenly it's gone.

It occurs to M that, should he want to, he could kill the two boys in their sleep. He would only need to steal upon the tent and open fire. It would be easy. But not worthwhile – until he has his tiger he must move like a ghost, unstoppable, and only if the boys proved a real threat would he need to consider jeopardising the hunt. And that time has not come, and he need cross no bridge unless he comes to it. With that thought in mind M turns away from the makeshift hacienda and sets off for his own sleeping spot, a spot selected earlier in the daylight hours, and – as bone-tiredness overcomes him – he starts counting in order to stay awake.

Bike, the boy who counts. None of it, realises M, can be forgotten. He can try to defile the past, the body can replenish all its cells every seven odd years, but somehow memory survives, persists. Bike, the boy who counts — what is he doing now? Where does he sleep? Does he lie awake at night in a strange room, with a poster on the wall that he doesn't like, and wait open-eyed for dawn? And what does the day bring: schoolyard taunts — your mother's in the loony bin — and after school, what then? A foster mother who hesitates before reaching out to touch him, a new sister or brother who takes him aside and reminds him that he will never, ever, be one of them?

To quash this uncomfortable train of fabrication M immerses himself in the utter present: Breathing in I calm myself, breathing out I smile, living in the present moment, happy in the present moment. He does not believe in this mantra, but he repeats it over and over because it dulls the pain.

Observations on the hacienda continue. The boys, as suspected, spend the day smoking and lounging around: Small throws a fishing line into the tarn and waits for Godot. At night M again steals close to catch their conversation, this time with more daring because he knows the boys' fuzzy state of mind. He cuts between the cover of rocks, exposed for a good ten metres, walking with the confidence of a shoplifter and trusting the boys won't hear him and turn around. Safe! He is so close now he can make out the lettering on a discarded packet of pasta: Fettucine Boscaiola. Fettucine Boscaiola . . . Nothing happens; M finds he is immune to the pleasures of warm Italian food.

With a sense of wonder Tall lists all the Hollywood actresses he knows who've had boob-jobs. When he gets to Helena Bonham-Carter, Small interjects, says it can't be so. Tall insists, Small shakes his head. Eventually they agree to disagree. 'Twenty dollars' worth,' says Small. 'Yeah, alright,' says Tall. And on it goes . . . Will they even mention the thylacine? thinks M. Does she even cross their minds? Sitting there, out of sight, spying on two fools, he begins to think he is wasting his time. The night is so black, the stars so many, the plateau so immense, any measures M might take to find the tiger seem hopelessly small. Should he leave the boys to their banter? It is tempting, but he knows it is safer to depart after they have fallen asleep. Patience, he tells himself, have patience.

Have patience, he tells himself, as two hours later Small launches into a lengthy diatribe about Darwin and his dangerous ideas . . . As soon as he can, M goes.

He has traps to set, things to do. It feels good to be up and walking around after all that sitting, and he swings his arms up and down, both at the same time, as if he were carving out a canoe around him. He stretches his Achilles tendons until a faint pain lets him know he is alive. Harrr, his breath turns hoary white. And on, as birds rouse and the tarns momentarily colour pink, he leaves the little tent behind. Rain falls, then stops. Should he sleep? Yes, he decides it would be wise to catch a few hours' rest before the long day ahead. He looks for a sleeping spot and soon finds one: a tree-fern has died and its fronds droop down to form a low natural tent. Shuffle under, wriggle in.

Even when sleeping M is semi-alert, guarding himself like Argus. A noise, far away and barely audible, floats by and because it is an unfamiliar sound his guard rallies, tries to decipher and, having failed to crack the code, reaches deep inside to shake his charge awake. What's that? Am I dreaming? A noise made by a machine: high-pitched, insistent. Then it's over, leaving no trace, as if it had never happened. He wants to believe it never happened, and only days ago he could have happily been persuaded. But not now, not today, and so lying there beneath the fern he tries to pinpoint the source of the mystery sound. If I were a thylacine, he thinks, it would read like a neon billboard. In the end it is not his aural sensitivity which guides him, but his reasoning: the machine sound came from the east, not the west, the boys are camped in the east, ergo the sound came from the boys' camp. Ah! A satellite communications system! Quick, up then – perhaps word of the tiger has come through!

By the time he reaches the campsite the boys have packed up and gone. This excites him. He follows their tracks and is surprised at how quickly they are travelling and in what direction. If they follow this course for long they will head out of the animal's home range into new and unfamiliar territory. He remembers: all animals are

154

essentially unpredictable, they are mysteries and not puzzles which can be worked out. A sobering thought: I would never have thought to come this way. Growing tired, he hopes the boys decide to stop and rest. Come midday and he sees no sign of two packs being laid down, and the afternoon passes in much the same way. They must be keen, he thinks, and hurries on.

Dusk. He must come upon them soon. Night. At last, he hears something. Up ahead, through the trees, is a flickering point of light: the fuel stove. Quietly, quietly now. Get close.

'I'm starving,' says Small, stirring a saucepan. 'Smells good.'

'You split, I choose,' says Tall.

'Yeah, OK.'

'Stick 'em up,' says Tall, levelling a gun at Small.

'Put that thing down.'

Tall tries to balance the butt of the gun on his outstretched palm. It is, sees M, a thick-barrelled tranquilliser gun.

Small heaps some pasta onto the lid of his saucepan. 'Here y'are.'

'You know,' says Tall, 'I reckon that even if I found the bloody thing I wouldn't tag it.'

'I know.'

'I'd hold it by the muzzle and point its nose dead west and tell the poor thing to run like the wind.'

'Take a photo first, but.'

'Yeah, I'd take a good photo, sell it for a few grand alright. Go to India.'

'Mate, you'd get a truckload of cash. I'd go to Chiang Mai.'

'Chiang Mai?'

'Yeah, Chiang Mai.'

'OK, deal, whoever takes the photo divvies up the money.'

'Yeah, OK, fair enough.'

'Deal then?'

'Deal, brother.'

The three of them migrate south-east for another four days. M's physiographic maps no longer help him (it is the return trip which needs to be kept in mind), and he faces a white border which marks the vacuous end of the world. But the next world, he sees, offers more of the same: he is standing in an expansive lichen-rich rock field, beyond which lies yet another swell of stunted woodland. Studying a new map, where bluffs and tiers and peaks have been scaled down to half their previous size and where a lack of detail leaves room for the sea-dragons beloved of ancient cartographers, he thinks of the thylacine and how she has wandered. Spatial memory, he knows, is a genetic thing, genetic and also learned. Perhaps she travelled this way years ago, sniffing by her mother's side. What fabulous combination of the senses, he wonders, lets her navigate without a map? If I were to return to my hometown – have mercy – would I, too, be able to get by on memory alone? As an exercise he journeys back to his childhood house, out onto the verandah, turns left down the street, past the Smiths' and the Tormeys', past the corner store, then right, heading towards the school, into Claremichael Street, past the church, through the vacant lot ... until he reaches the brown wooden fence which runs paling by paling, twenty-seven in all, right up to the school gate.

The boys are still travelling with no concern that they might be being followed, like cows who are shadowed by birds in the paddock, or campers trailed by devils, this is the easy natural order of things. See, a dirt-brown boot-print smack in the middle of a cushion plant; piles of unburied shit dotted like cairns. On they go, until at last they string their hammock up and make themselves at home. Watching, watching. Small cooks the pasta and Tall shouts 'Aloha Chiang Mai!'. Tonight M is hungry – in four days all he has eaten are a few raw eggs lifted from a nest. In the early morning the boys leave their packs behind and go off searching, during which time M takes the opportunity to peruse their site, examine their stuff. They have enough food, he calculates, to last for another week and he wonders if they plan a return trip or if they are expecting a delivery of supplies. He steals a block of hard cheese, a bag of scroggin and a bag of dried fruit, not caring if they might be missed. Inside the orange tent he looks for the gun and camera but cannot find them. Quickly, quickly – scurry away. Sitting himself under a rock ledge he nibbles the cheese, works it around in his mouth. Early explorers ravaged by hunger tried to eat their clothing; another party survived by bleeding one another and drinking the blood from a shoe. He admires other men's endurance, chews.

———

During the days the boys search for the tiger; M hunts and avoids the boys and any of the other National Parks crew who may have converged on the area. And the tiger, what does she do? Lives, breathes, eats and shelters . . . M guesses she is oblivious to her new-found fame.

He finds a lair. Strictly speaking, he does not know if it is a lair, because the zoologists were always uncertain as to whether the thylacine actually used one spot for rearing pouch young, but at the very least he knows he has found a bolthole, a safe house. And the more he scrutinises the site, the more excited he becomes. The two sloping side walls of the lair (lair, he wants to call it a lair) are formed by two oddly shaped ironstone boulders, one waist-high and the other higher again. They are touching so that no rain can squeeze between the two. From the front it looks as if the crevice is small and shallow, but this is not the case. Instead the narrow opening is the tip of a triangle, and the lair runs back in a V-shape for almost two metres until it hits a high dirt bank. This deceptive opening is in turn disguised by the surrounding scrub and other nearby impenetrable rock falls. He did not find it immediately, this lair, was not drawn to it by a mysterious sixth sense or siren call. A cache of bones – frail bird bones, wallaby skulls and a tumble of rodent bones – piled under a rock ledge some fifteen metres away had been the first indication that the tiger might have passed this way. He had scoured the surrounds for a good four hours, working in that realm beyond time (four hours? maybe five or six), egged on by a stiff and dry twisted scat which might or might not have come from his tiger, knowing there was fresh water and a feeding ground close at hand (all the signs were there), until – leaving no stone unturned – he had stuck his head into the crevice and – behold! Aladdin's den!

There is enough daylight to take a good look around. Down on his knees on the well-tamped earthen floor, M sniffs various levels of the air and determines on smell alone that it is clear an animal has used this lair in the recent past. His first treasure: hairs. A selection of short stiff brown hairs; a few lighter brown hairs of equal length; and one longer darker hair that could have come from the tip of a tail. His second treasure – hidden in a far corner and illuminated by torchlight – his second treasure is so alarmingly beautiful that he touches it as he would the Holy Grail or his own first child. Bones of a pup, pale and clean, undisturbed since the creature lay down to die: the narrow small skull fallen off the cervical vertebrae at a quizzical angle, a scatter of teeth. This could not be the pup of his own tiger, the state of decay is too well advanced for that, but rather the remains of an unknown great-aunt or uncle. So, lonesome, is this where she comes for company? M trails a finger over the curved lumpy spine, then he lies down on the ground in a mirror position, eye to eye with the skull, and imagines for a second that he,

159

too, will rot in this cave. In years to come, decades later, an intrepid explorer will find the skeletons and ponder the relationship between the two.

He will lie in wait. That's what he will do. At night the thylacine will hunt her own prey and some time, one day, she will return to her lair for sleep and company. He will make his home between the boulders, cover the floors with warm wallaby skins. Yes, he thinks, I could be quite comfortable here.

He grows old.

He takes to carving designs into bones from the cache using the point of his knife; it is fine intricate work, well suited to the art of waiting. In time he has quite a collection lined up like fence posts at the back of his lair. And when his eye is caught by a splash of red on a fallen feather, or – on rare occasions – by a colourful wildflower bloom, he brings them home for his own edification. He lets his beard curl and grow. Sitting out a heavy storm he decides that the word 'rain' is so inadequate a description of the variable manifestations of precipitation that it is almost useless, and to amuse himself he makes up new, better words: 'apitrition' – when, during a steady fall, the rain picks up in one particular area before dying back down to its steady rate soon after. But this tack, the inadequacy of language, leads him down a slippery slope, until he is almost persuaded never to talk again. Like some kind of monk.

Throughout this waiting he tends to the duties of survival

with professional care. The boys he checks on regularly, and when one day he discovers their site empty, tent gone, he is not surprised. A quick survey shows they intend to return: they have filled their hammock with gear and strung it out of harm's way high in the fork of a tree. Good, he is pleased they have gone, for now he can cook his meat at any hour of the day without concern that they will catch its smell. Meat – the happy butcher – opposite Ye Old Tudor Hotel – there is not one second when M envies his rivals their recreational trip to town.

—

He is asleep, curled up in the lair. Today the sky is a clear sharp blue and the world becalmed. It is a day of clarity. He has been asleep for some hours now, sleeping without dreaming, cells popping and other scavenger cells rushing in to clean up the mess.

So sleep.

And because he is the natural man, who can see and hear and smell what other men cannot, he finds this sleep needled and disturbed. Crossing the threshold into consciousness he realises that he is hearing something – a rustling outside, movement. And because he is diligent and committed to his work he summons superhuman energy and rolls over onto his belly, sticks his face out and takes a look. Disappearing in the direction of the cache of bones is – he catches sight of the back end of a dun-brown black-striped animal the size of a large dog, all thin and tattered

161

looking. Instantly, chemically, he is alert. His view is obscured by foliage, but this – this is it – he knows what he has seen . . .

He crawls out of the lair, rifle slung over his shoulder. The air outside is cooler, the light brighter. He knows what to do, and he knows that he can do it, an army general with the hard skill of a foot soldier. He moves with as much speed as stealth can afford, taking care not to unsettle loose rocks or crack fallen branches. On this route he will come around to the animal's eating spot, at the same time blocking off the most likely avenue of escape. He calculates that she will run away from the lair, and not toward it. He wants her to run to him.

The thylacine is sunning herself on a slab of rock, shovelling her pointed wolf-like face into the bloody remains of a wallaby. M watches, fascinated. It is because of the wallaby, he thinks, that she hasn't smelt me; her nostrils are overwhelmed. He has his gun jammed up against one eye and his finger married to the cold steel trigger, but still he watches. She pauses in her guzzling, stretches out her back by lifting her hindquarters. Then she settles down to feed again. What he is seeing is both beautiful and terrible at the same time, and he watches with the same rapt attention he would devote to a film which told the story of his own life, past and future. There is no way he will miss this shot, and he holds the animal in his sights, knowing that he is a killer, and that he, too, will be killed. Part of him wants to keep watching, perhaps even walk away, but another part fixes him there, poised and ready, and it is the part of him he recognises as strong and true.

Perhaps it was a breeze so subtle he didn't even feel it, or perhaps it was her innate instinct for survival, whatever the case, the thylacine jerks her head up from the carcass and vigorously sniffs the air. Then she is up on her feet, her rounded ears pricked upright and her fur hackled. Her stringy body is taut and well sprung. Slowly she surveys her surrounds, and he watches, exhilarated, as her gaze cruises past him. His heart thumps inside his chest and he makes an effort to take slow measured breaths. Then snap, suddenly she is staring straight at him, eyes wide, and he watches as her cavernous jaw cleaves open and he listens to an unholy strangled hissing roar.

He shoots as soon as she starts to leap and the first bullet catches her mid-air. The second and third bullets, fired in quick succession, bring her to the ground.

And that is it.

Now the whole world has exploded; startled birds sound the death knell. He leaves his cover and lets the gun hang down by his side. The thylacine is lying with her back toward him, curled like a sleeping dog. She's not dead yet. If I didn't know better, thinks M, I'd say she was giving suck to her young. He approaches cautiously, as if by some miracle she might have another life to call upon. Drawing close he can hear her wheezing, see her shudder intermittently. And just as he had been compelled to watch before, he finds himself unable to do the right thing now and finish her off. Ancient words which might once have helped him, words big enough for the beautiful terribleness of the deed, are long lost and out of reach, so he says, whispers, the best he can think of, which is – simply – you won't die alone.

He circles tight, until he can look into her eyes. They are a deep yellowy-brown and when he does look into them he realises that she in turn does not seem to see him – her eyes are blank and vacant and say nothing. The jaw is distended; black rubbery folds of skin hide pink-brown gums, the gums hold coated oval teeth. The hair on her face is a whitish-brown. Quickly, and without thinking, he lifts his rifle and shoots her in the head.

Kneeling down, he rests his hand against the fine creamy fur that shields her bony chest – nothing. Testing himself, he gingerly puts one hand inside the gaping jaw and, afraid, quickly pulls it out again. She is more than an animal to him, more than a wallaby or pademelon, and he observes her body as he would the body of a friend laid out in the morgue. It galls him that he can press a finger against her wet nose, that he can close her eyes: it feels so wrong. She looks nothing like the creature he knew before. There is an impassable, unimaginable gulf between life and death, so that even life at its lowest ebb, lying ill or morose, barely moving, such life is utterly vibrant when compared to death. Now, her stillness is obscene.

He knows what he has to do. To protect the body from scavengers and searchers he constructs a shroud from branches, adding a cover of leaves. He quickly returns to the lair to fetch his pack. Walking back to the site he thinks only of the task before him, how it will be unpleasant, but how it must be done. Then, to give himself the best chance of performing well, he repeats the mantra which anchors him to the absolute present: Breathing in I calm myself, breathing out I smile ... Until there he is, the thylacine lying before him just as he had left her. He thinks: If I had walked away, and if there were no devils, she would lie like this day after day, through storms and rain, letting snakes slither over her, unblinking. Marvelling at the extraordinary patience of the dead, he suddenly decides he will be cremated when he dies.

From his pack he unearths the surgical kit. Snap, on go the translucent rubber gloves that turn his hands to wax. Step two: he unrolls his green cloth and checks all his tools are there. Then he rolls the animal onto her back, not an easy job, but she refuses to balance and flops back over onto her side. He removes his shaver from its sterile packaging and, with one shoulder, pushes back a haunch, exposing the inner groin, and shaves an envelope-sized patch above the femoral artery; he does this carefully, like a mother tenderly brushing the hair of a murder victim. He collects the hair in a small sterile plastic snaplock jar. For a split second he wonders if one day he will go bald – stop it. The next bit is the bit he does not like, and he instructs himself as he would a younger cadet: Get the blood, don't be ridiculous, just get the blood. Under instruction he disinfects the shaved patch with an alcohol solution and then unwraps a needle and syringe. He twists the needle into the base of the syringe and checks that it is tight. Like a watchmaker, he holds his handiwork up to the light. It is the needle which disturbs him, not the blood itself – for some reason he can't bear the thought of sliding a needle into the vein and surreptitiously drawing out the blood. To shoot and cut and gash, that is forthright – it is the stealth of the needle he dislikes. Calm now, calm: Breathing in I calm myself, breathing out I smile . . . Piercing the skin and taking care not to jab right through the vein, he watches as a dark drop of blood washes back into the base of the needle. In! Don't move a muscle. He pulls on the syringe at a steady glacial pace until the cylinder is full, then he withdraws the needle, and transfers its dark contents to a test tube bearing an opalescent glob of heparin; the test tube he cradles in a titanium cold-pack. He does this ten times, each time with the same level of discomfort and efficiency.

And now the obstetrics, which is more his style. He cuts into the groin and slides a hand in to search for the ovaries ... searching, searching. When he has them he locks each one away in a custom-built vial of liquid nitrogen, handling the nitrogen as if it were a bomb. An egg, he knows, can be fertilised with the sperm of a semi-compatible organism, like a lynx or a wolf. Or, better still, but needing more time, a sperm could be fashioned from the thylacine's own blood. Self-impregnation. He pulls out the uterus – intact – a plump slippery slimy thing. There is little or no chance it contains a foetus, but he takes it just the same; not to do so would be remiss. Then the job is done; the motherlode safely packed away.

The job is done. The job is almost done.

Still wearing his rubber gloves he moves his pack away from the carcass (when it became a carcass he isn't sure, but the bloody gutted thing is no longer a body to him). Next – destroy the evidence, ensure no-one else can access the material. Only he will have it, he will be the only one. Building a pyre with the branches, lifting the limp carcass onto the pyre, he tells himself that he is the only one: The only one, I am the only one. This thought grows light in him, incandescent. All the energy of the sun runs through him and into the earth; he is the source of all animation. Petrol-blue flames lick up over the pyre, and burn and burn and burn. And burn, until the focal point of the dirty black smoke could be anything at all. M pours water over the blackened bones, carries them into the scrub and, working up a sweat, buries them deep beneath the ground.

There, now he is the only one.

He did not expect to cross paths with the boys, and so is surprised when he sees two figures drop out of the line of gums and amble toward him through the button-grass. There is no point trying to escape, he has clearly been spotted. Tall raises a hand in the way all compatriots do when encountering another human in an isolated place. As the boys approach he sees they have on a fresh change of clothes and both are clean-shaven, and he decides, almost immediately, that if he has to, he will shoot them. Nothing

167

personal, he will do it as a last resort. Now, prepare yourself. He is glad he has rinsed himself of the worst excesses, the blood and slime, although he worries – irrationally, yes – that what he carries will give him away, that it will emit a high-frequency sound, or glow like a radioactive sample. Call for help.

Here they come: stay calm.

'Oh hey, it's you,' says Small.

The two boys look him over, and by the expression on their faces M can tell he must be a sight – ragged, unkempt, with the gait of a predator. That won't do, he will have to jolly them along.

'Hello again.'

'You alright, man?' asks Tall.

'Fine, no problem. Just coming to the end of a long haul.'

'Devils – research, wasn't it?' says Small.

'That's right.'

'Crafty buggers. Get what you wanted?'

'Just about. Where are you headed?'

'Over that way,' says Tall, pointing – divining – in the direction of the lair.

'It's beautiful, man, the tiger hunt. We just hang around up here getting paid by the day.'

'Do you think you'll find one? I mean, don't they say –'

'That's exactly right, but believe it or not, man, word is a guy got a good, long look at one, no joke, not that long ago, man,' says Tall.

'She's real alright,' confirms Small. 'Hallelujah, you'd better believe it.'

'Well, good luck then.'

'Thanks, man. Hey, no offence but you don't look too good. Are you sure you're OK? We've got a special radio thing, we could –'

'No problem, boys, really, I'm heading straight back.'

'Terrible, wasn't it?' says Small, pointedly, and when M fails to answer, adds, 'About the Armstrongs.'

'Yes, terrible, surprising, really.'

There is an awkward pause which is not so much a sign of respect but rather what happens when none of them is able to summon a social grace which can accommodate grief and all the other things known to be truly bad.

'Poor girl,' says Tall eventually, 'at her age.'

'Terrible,' repeats M.

'And poor bloody Bike – what a nutcase that kid was.'

'Yeah, well, touch wood,' says Small, knocking on Tall's skull.

Mention of the Armstrongs is now as foreign to M as mention of another planet; he knows it exists, that it has subtle but powerful effects, that it is very far away. Only Bike is real to him, Bike – the boy who counts.

'How about some food, then?' Small looks to Tall for brotherly confirmation.

'Yeah, man, we've got plenty.'

Before M can reply Small rolls his pack off his shoulders and fishes around inside.

'*Voilà!*' Two fresh oranges. He thrusts them forward.

Now M stands clumsily with an orange in each hand.

'A quick cup of tea?' asks Tall.

'No thanks, got a fair way to go.'

'Hey!' exclaims Small, scrabbling around under M's feet. 'Hey! Check this out!'

What! The boy has seen blood, smelt it – so, ready now. If necessary he will calmly drop his pack, assemble his rifle, aim and shoot.

But there is no need. Small holds in his palm for all to see a gleaming little white block of quartzite, an anomalous sight on the dolerite plateau. Closing his hand he tosses the rock into the grass so that for two seconds, maybe three, it tumbles over and over, and for those two or three seconds it is a miraculous new thing: a rock in air. The three of them watch it disappear.

'So,' says M, 'I'll be seeing you then.'

'OK, man.'

'Yeah, *adios amigo*.'

When M walks away he doesn't turn to see if he is being watched. He walks with his back straight, picking his way through the clumps of button-grass and swinging the oranges he still carries in each hand. The sun breaks from behind a reef of clouds and this cheers him, although he knows the sun does not shine for one man alone. Checking his watch he sees that he hasn't long before night falls and, wanting to reach his buried coffee, his sweet warm hidden coffee, Martin David sighs and adjusts his precious cargo, hurries on.